Snake

Edward Arruns Mulhorn

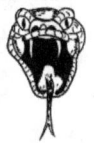

Sweet is the swamp with its secrets,
Until we meet a snake;
'Tis then we sigh for houses,
And our departure take

At that enthralling gallop
That only childhood knows.
A snake is summer's treason,
And guile is where it goes

The Swamp, Emily Dickinson

The Chinese Year of the Snake

Snakes are deep thinkers and always mysterious, possessing the power to bewitch. Born under the sign of wisdom, they are intelligent and wise, though this intellect is restless. Snakes are graceful and softly spoken, calm by nature, but intense. Cautious and guarded, they tend to analyse a situation before jumping into it. They trust themselves above all others, and in that they are seldom wrong. They hate to fail at anything, so are fired with intense determination. Once they have made a mistake, they never repeat it. By nature, they are skeptical beings, but they keep their suspicions to themselves. They are very private, and idle gossip is not for them. Despite being seductive and alluring, they are frequently unlucky in love. One can never tell how far snakes will go to achieve their aims. They are relentless and they never stop plotting. When angered, one feels their icy hostility instead of hearing sharp words. They always appear docile and quiet, and they never betray their true feelings. Their moves are planned out well in advance, and they bide their time for revenge. They can be evasive, and just when they seem to be caught, they slip away and are gone. They are subtle workers, imperceptibly manoeuvering and manipulating until they are ready to get what they want. Whatever happens, snakes always strike out for themselves. They know how to use people and situations to their advantage.

The Ley

Earth. The body of land a curvaceous shape clothed with irregular fields. The seams of its dress thick hedges of earth, covered in bramble and sedge. The dress itself, a rainbow of green, windswept and raw, hugging the pregnant roll of the land, close-fitted around its arching shoulders, its ribs, the mould of its neck. The dress it wears is studded with jewels – a clutch of sheep, a gang of crows, the manoeuvrings of an aimless pheasant. And then, sprung from nothing and awkwardly clinging, the occasional lump of a house. Clumps of bush are huddled in valleys; elsewhere solitary trees stand hunchbacked, distorted and gnarled by the wind. The tails of the dress are frayed and unkempt, dissolving into bracken and gorse as it strives to hide the limbs of the cliff crudely poking beneath it. This is the land.

Water. Washing against the body of land, in ceaseless movement, a giddy mass, endless and formless and grey, melting into the liquid ether as it stretches out beyond sight. Shapeless, yet matching every shape. Forming itself into infinite beings for elusive fractions of time. Restless, resistless, colourless. Murmuring the smoothest caress, inducing eternal slumber. Then screaming nightmare, pounding the land, venting its unspoken fury. A rippling gloss which harbours life – a teeming world unseen beyond the splintered teeth of the rock. Dancing a bolero to the rhythm of the moon. This is the sea.

Wind. Fire. And here – couched in a valley of the body, earth, its head in the lap of its mother, the sea – is the ley. At its neck is a slow stream, brown and deep, which wends through the bank of sand on the beach, becoming thinner and more transparent as it meets with the salt of the sea. At the base of its neck are two walls of dune, thick with startled grass. It reaches out a mile inland – an oily half-river covered in reed – dissolving to field as the valley flattens, as its brackish waters drain away. At its fringe, and tracing a rough-cut line, crouching bushes and scratches of sedge mark its boundary with the fields.

At dawn, a low mist blankets the ley, ghosting the squatting bushes grey and the reeds a damp cold silver. Breezes cut above its head, teasing the uppermost tassels. Within the quietness of its core, random birds bob careless flight, and cling to the shivering reeds. Tentative rays reach over the hill, stretching into the heart of the ley, defining it, giving it colour and shape. The reeds take form, green-silver and brown, and then are burnished to bloodied red as the mist burns off their brittle backs, as they stand in the glory of the sun. At its neck, the ley is alive with sound, singing a shivering lament with no words, dancing a trance in the wind. Further inland, the reeds are thin, swaying but slightly, in unison, murmuring a ceaseless rosary through tight, invisible lips. By day, the ley endures the light, absorbing it, blocking it out from its heart. The brackish waters never warm, nor laze in the gaze of the sun. At dusk, the ley shrugs off its shape. Yet still it breathes; and still it waits. Alive. Forever awake.

In winter months, the sea rears up, spewing its salt in the mouth of the ley, forcing it open to drink of it deep, till its sullen waters are stirred to life. Leaden skies empty their spiteful load as they meet with the barren land. Rain spins off the polished fields; it chases down the contoured slopes, till the reeds are choked and drowned.

Broad channels of brackish water emerge to furrow the face of the ley. A furious wind scratches its surface. The reeds crease in agony, bowing submissive, caught in an unrelenting slaughter, screaming a bitter wretchedness that severs their skin and chills to the soul.

In summer, the ley scarcely meets with the sea. The waters are brown and void of movement, receding into the base of the reeds, where shadows lie waiting to cool it. The reedbed thickens. Slender fresh shoots, ecstatically green, pierce through the mudbed, aimed at the sky. The sun scorches the tips of the sweltering reeds; it bronzes the curtains of the ley – the bushes and the tinder scrub – till the valley appears to catch fire. The ley grows pregnant with waiting life, sweating and sighing a warm embrace between the thighs of the field. Here, in the fulsome eye of the sun, the ley swoons, outwardly still.

Yet within its core there is constant motion: the pulse of a beating heart. The ley is life; it nurtures life. The markings of warrens are scratched on the slopes. The trace of a path is cut through the sedge, shaped by the tread of a badger. Otters and mink are hid in its depths. Voles and shrews befriend its banks. Adders and lizards sun on stones which bulge from the land like blisters. A grass snake swims in the stagnant water, dipping its head as it dives for food. Frogs, newts and speckled toads are buried alive within the sludge of the mudbed. Bats weave and circle over its head; butterflies wend haphazard routes; honeybees brood; dragonflies hover, pulsing the air with their fragile wings. And birds, everywhere. The sleek sand martin angling flight as it shimmies through the close-set reeds; the yellow wagtail courting mates with baffled feathers and shivering wings; the grasshopper warbler, heard but not seen; the bearded reedling with her brown-streaked eggs in a nest of leaves lined with flowers. The meadow pipit, surfing through tiers of blue sky, singing while sliding to earth. A kingfisher, perched on a broken bulrush, nodding its head and flicking its tail before plunging into the water to feed. An imperious buzzard, high above all, surveying the commotion of life.

Man alone is the single creature unable to carve a living from this. This is no place for man. On either side of the ley are fences: fierce defences erected by those who consciously choose to be exiled. Houses overlook from a distance: watchful, respectful, but wary. A single dwelling, charred and in ruins, lies within the rim of the fence.

Free from the clutch of curious man, the ley is a turbulent wilderness. A prison, a paradise. A labyrinth of reed, where creatures search and stumble blind. A shock of sudden pools and potholes; of natural traps and snares. An isolation; an eternity. Thrashed by the wind, burned by the sun, mocked by the chattering reeds. A place of death, of things once drowned, of things that have decayed. Yet from decay is born new life. A cycle of renewal, rebirth. Ageless and timeless, and without end.

Not earth nor water. Somewhere between. This is a borderland. A land forged from the bowels of earth and sculpted into miraculous being. A micro world. A part of the real world, living apart. Bowing to seasons, to wind and to fire, to the shocks that nature thrusts upon it. Resistant to the will of man. Cold, uncomfortable, close, confined. A solitude. Host to a universe entire, which lives and thrives, survives and dies, feeding off its own.

This is the ley.

The Girl

Her hair was unruly and dark. It defied both brushes and combs. There were always things in it – things that were caught there. Things that were meant to be there, like bunches, and things that weren't meant to, like straw. How could she find straw in the city? And yet she did, for there it was, trapped in the snare of her locks. Her hair was thick. In an effort to tame it, they cut it short to her shoulders. They cut it every month. Then, for almost an hour perhaps, she would be the child that her parents wanted, before her hair returned to the wild, and she became the thing that she was – an innocent child, a child of nature, a child moulded of clay.

Her skin was weathered and tough, as though belonging to someone much older. Her face was unusually pale and cold. She had a flat brow, a sloping nose, a pointed chin. Her eyes were darkest green. They watched you, watched you, watched you always. Always wide and never blinking. Her lips were thin and dull.

She was sinewy and nimble. She could climb a tree using only her arms, pulling herself through the boughs. She could hang from bars by her hands. And, when she chose, she could hang from bars by only her feet, wrapping her arms round her chest like a bat. She was fast and fearless. She had balance and strength that gave her a freedom to go in directions beyond what was known. Beyond where others would think of going, beyond where they wanted or needed to go. Her toes were long, like little fingers. She wriggled and squirmed; she couldn't be held.

She wore bright-coloured dresses printed with flowers, prettily tied with laces and bows. And under her dress she wore jeans that were frayed, with earth in their pockets and mud on their knees. When outside, the dress was hitched in her belt so she could run and climb and be free. So she could ride on the back of the wind, so she could glide on the air.

She was ten years old, and born in the year of the snake.

Her parents were professional people. They had been drawn to London separately, in search of career and success. In London they had found their calling, in London they had found each other, in London they had got married. Now they were wed, they were rooted to London. It was where they belonged, it was all they required. It was where they had sunk all their hope. It was their singular promise, their future, their now. In London they lived, in a pleasant house which was bound by a garden six yards square.

They had started a family with the same careful planning as expressed in their salaried lives. They had thought to raise a couple of children, to apportion being a parent between them, to balance the ambition they held for their work with the time they invested in their upcoming offspring, in the hope of fulfilment in both.

That ambition had been tested early. The structure they sought to impose on the girl was challenged by the thing that she was. They continually had to adapt, to concede, when managing both of these worlds. Balance forever proved elusive, and in tending to this creature they nurtured, both felt the frustration of sacrifice.

Sitting at home, the mother knew there were projects at work she couldn't take on, meetings she couldn't attend. There were people she couldn't influence, promotion that went other ways. Sometimes, from somewhere deep inside, a disquiet would surface that she couldn't disguise. Having a child – for all its joy – had set her back by two years. The mother struggled to resist this fact. It grew on her as a reluctant resentment, a subversive truth, weaving through her fabric of life, tainting her bond with the girl.

For his part, the father showed willing to acquire the skills of nappy-changing, buggy-folding, bottle-warming, sick-removal. He had been through ante-natal class; he had been through post-natal depression; he had been through random panic attacks that left him holding the child in his arms in unwelcome places at unpleasant times. But for all he might involve himself, he became aware – as reality settled into routine – of how parenting lacks parity, and of his own subordinate role. Under the bitter truth of this knowledge he focused himself on his job, aware that he was also resented: resented for simply leaving the house, resented for simply going to work, which – no matter how arduous nor tedious it was – would be seen by his wife as a chance for himself, as an excuse to escape from the child.

If a child can bring a couple together, it can also tear them apart. The girl unwittingly sparked a discord, simply by coming into existence, simply by being and continuing to be. Buried in the unspeakable, the parents knew their daughter's birth had compromised both of their lives. However they sought to ignore or disguise it, from others and even sometimes from themselves, some of this implicit truth may have spilled its light on the girl.

As has to be, routine began to establish itself. It started to manage the scope of their days; it shifted its pattern to shape and fit their lives as they changed and evolved. The girl was ever an early riser, awakening with the sun. As an infant she would stand at her window watching the creep of the dawn; and, when old enough to go downstairs, she would open the doors and run onto the lawn.

She was independent from a very young age, as if she was conscious of the distance between them, as if she was conscious of their distance from her. Yet solitude was her sanctuary. At the break of each day, she would stand in the garden, watchful, acute to all that was in it, till her parents came down to the kitchen. Then they packed her bag and took her away – to a carer, to crèche, to school. She lived in these other worlds by day, returning only at dusk. To stand in the garden until it was supper, until she was called up to bed. On the weekends she fashioned a world of her own, living it mostly unseen. Her parents played with her sometimes then, but she seemed so content, so at ease with herself, they often let her alone.

As a child, the days and the nights were all hers. They were hers alone, and she spent them alone. While she was small, she felt this seclusion to be her salvation. But, as she grew, she grew resentful. Resentful to be where she was. Though her parents might have thrived in London, for her it became a constraint. A place where she was denied. With a garden too small to run or to hide in. Where she couldn't escape and be free.

This furious desire for freedom grew stronger the more that the parents strove to contain it. From seeds of frustration it bred like a canker, infecting all that she did.

Her pale white skin turned pallid and cold; her huge eyes stared from her listless face. She closed herself down, she closed off the world. Sometimes she seemed not to breathe. At last, as if life was being sucked from her, as if she had lost the spirit to live, she begged her parents for the space to draw air. Here she was trapped; here she was starving. She was drowning, dissolving away.

Her parents were scared. They had never witnessed such strength of being, such passion before in a child. They retreated from outright rejection to reason, and then they gave in to the girl. They agreed to go for a long weekend, to a cottage close to the sea. The parents hoped it would meet her desire, while the girl was possessed by the promise it gave. The wild, the untamed, the unknown.

A train ride and a hire car later, they found themselves in sobering darkness miles from the safety of home. Her father cut the engine. For a moment, no one stirred. The girl sat, restless, in the back of the car, holding her breath, unwilling to breathe. Unable to see beyond the window – beyond her pale, reflected face – into the void of night. Then she opened her door. She stepped onto the drive.

She could see nothing. Nothing but the frame of a garage lit by a dull light stamped on its forehead, and the shadow of hedges beyond. She could see nothing; but leaning back and closing her eyes, she felt moist drops of rain on her face, she felt a cool wind stinging her skin. She could smell the salt, she could sense there was life – life in the thicket, in the fields beyond, and, further still, in the sea. In the sea which turned and turned again, ceaselessly in the never distance. And, more acutely than ever before, she felt herself coming alive.

The next morning, the girl arose with the sun. She went out into the melting garden, still sweating and stung by the midnight dew. By the time her parents called her to breakfast, she knew that garden by heart. That day, though the broad fields tempted her to them – and there in the distance, there was the sea – she reined in her will and promised herself to keep her universe tight. She sat cross-legged beside a hydrangea, close to a bank which held the garden free from encroaching fields. She closed her eyes and spread her fingers, resting her opened hands on her thighs, her palms laid upwards and scorched by the sun. She didn't move; she couldn't see; she lost herself to the sense of touch. She could feel a butterfly on her neck; she could feel another land in her hair. She could hear them settling and launching themselves. She could hear the motion of flight. She could feel them spreading their delicate wings, basking in the dazzling sun, burnished and speckled in splendour.

Round the back of a shed, on a shaded wall, she found a cluster of snails. Picking up three, she lay on her back, feeling the rub of the lawn. She raised her blouse so her tummy was bare; she placed the snails on her skin. She watched their bodies slowly expand; she felt the wash of their trail. She laid them in an invisible line, intrigued to see which slithered first to reach the luxurious grass.

She ran towards a stunted fir, clambering up the tangled boughs which laddered its cool and dim insides till she stood in the deep-set dusk of its heart. She peered through molten green swathes of stems towards splinters of radiant lawn. She measured time by gusts of wind, by the shifting shadow spread on the grass, by the fragile filters of light and shade which breathed its soul into life.

She returned to the cottage once that day. Only once. To pluck a spider from the bath in response to her mother's entreaty. She took him with her, cupped in her hands, outside. Outside. Into the wind, the light, the smell, the touch, the taste, the being, the breath, the living, the promise, the presence, the very essence of life.

At dusk the family ate. The girl sat nearest to the window, watching the garden shiver and smile; watching the crows as they pecked at nothing, as they chatted and huddled, and hopped low flight to the next dense patch of green. She watched the face of the massive sky drifting above her; she watched the spectral beings within it relentlessly shifting their shape. She screwed up her eyes to the blurry distance, seeking life on the grey-blue cliffs, seeking movement in amongst the colourless wash of the sea. She fooled herself that even here, sat inside behind the glass, she could hear the water breathing and sighing, sucking the air through its teeth.

The following morning, the girl persuaded her parents to go for a walk. They climbed a stile beside the drive, then stepped down into the wind-teased grass that bordered a planted field. She led them round the broken edge between the crop and the hedge. She heard the scrunch of her feet as they met with the skin of the crusted earth. She heard the lisp of the grass on her shins. She peered at the secret core of the verge; she stared at the fluttering sea of the field with big, believing eyes. She felt the clear air sharp on her face, the spotted warmth of the sun.

They clambered over a gate to a field rampant with weed which rose to her waist. And here, a rash of colours and smells rushed to bombard and assault her senses.

Immediate, intense, and shocked into life, then dissolving away on the breeze. The girl closed her eyes, steering by touch: by the give of the earth beneath her feet, by the shimmer of wind on her skin. She opened her hands, her palms faced downwards, inviting the whisper of grass, the rude crackle of stems. Feeling the pleasure and feeling the pain of being blind to the world. She stopped to listen. At a gasp of air; a shiver of grass; the harsh kiss of her parents' boots slicing through the tinder scrub; the distant breath of the sea. And deeper still – within her, beyond her, and all around – she could sense her own breath, her beating heart, the blood which pumped through her arteries, bringing her body alive. Alive, and transporting her into the sky. High, high above, in the invisible air, immersed in the sound of flickering wings.

When they came to a farther gate, they rested. The girl sat straddling the uppermost bar, while her parents stood to her side. In the hedge she could hear the mutterings of movement, the flutter of leaves, the frisson of breeze. Before them, a breadth of sloping earth – fields locked fiercely shoulder to shoulder, arching down to the bed of a valley, rising proud on the farther side. And farther still, she could see the sea. She saw it and smelt it and breathed it in. She breathed in this body beautiful, this rich, majestic land. She felt it washing upon her, inside her. She felt it melting into her skin; she felt it seeping into her flesh, until it fused with her bone. Till she and the gate, and the air – and all that she saw, and all that there was – had been intricately woven as one.

The girl twisted her body and looked to her side, aware that her parents had moved. They had turned their backs on all that she saw; they were walking away up the field.

They were going back towards the house. It seemed their walk was done for the day; their adventure had come to a close. It appeared it was time for them all to return.

How could that be? They had hardly begun. There was still so much to see, and to feel. There was the valley; the clutch of trees; the fields. And beyond them, not far in the distance, the sea. The sea. Surely, they wanted to go there too. Surely, they wanted to see.

The girl slid off the gate and ran to stand in their path. They met her protestations with smiles. They were ready to go to the cottage now. To have some coffee, to read the papers, to rest their legs for a while. Perhaps they could go out later, by car; perhaps they could visit the sea. The girl marched in their steps back over the field, back around the planted earth. The radiant sunshine all around her was withering, fading, shrinking to nothing, losing its texture and form. The thrill, the shock of life she had witnessed seemed to unravel before her.

The girl stood in the garden, alone. It was bigger, much bigger, than their garden at home. It was wilder, too, with more animals here than she knew the names of, or knew she could find. It was full of secrets, of living things, of things yet waiting to come alive. But it was still no more than a garden. It was not the landscape where they had just been — the wilderness fuelling such promise. Out there she had felt herself drowning in life. Just beginning to breathe, to be free. Just beginning to know, beginning to feel. But now, that moment was gone. Her parents were sitting content on a bench, with papers and coffee, exhausted. How could they sit there and squander their lives, with this brave new world to explore?

The girl stood in the cottage garden, unmoving, her back pressed tight to a bank. She knew that beyond it, over its mound, was the welcoming lie of a field. A field that was unplanted, untamed; that was urging her to explore. She tried to imagine herself within it, thinking of all she might find there. Imagining the smells and the touch. The mere sensation of wandering within it, of knowing herself to be free. It was no good. Without the need to open her eyes, she knew she was here in the garden. In a neat, trimmed, ordered plot of fenced earth. She was here, and not in the field. Why did she have to conjure a picture when it lay just beyond her, and she could be there, seeing it all for herself? When would she see it again? The girl's imaginings, though strong, were nothing beside her lust to see. And, as she climbed up onto the bank, as she let her body roll down its side, she told herself that she wouldn't go far, she wouldn't stay out for too long.

It was over an hour before the girl's parents realised their daughter had gone. The garden was big, and they had assumed the morning's walk was enough. They called her to lunch, then called her again. They found there was no response to their cries. No face at the window, no sound of her feet. So they lay down their papers and went outside. They walked round the garden casually; then again, with greater concern. A third time they called out, they called her by name. And only then was it clear to them both that their daughter was no longer there. In that fraction of frozen clarity, the absurdity of their expectations laid itself bare to them both. How could they have thought she would stay here – here, in a place without fences or locks, where the land which harboured such life and intrigue lay unchecked on all sides.

Please come back here. Come on now. Mummy's so worried about you.

I don't want to come back. I like it here.

If you come back, I'll give you something.

What?

Something you want.

Like what?

Whatever you want.

I want a pet.

We've been through that before.

I want a pet.

Please come back.

If you give me a pet.

Please come back here. Please.

Only if you buy me a pet.

The hamster's name was Flasher. It wasn't much of a pet as pets go, but it was warm and alive. It was hers. She called it Flasher because it ran fast. That, and because its eyes were red. Just like the eyes of a rat. It had a cage, but the girl soon taught it to live in a pouch which she hung from her shoulder and tucked into her chest. She carried the hamster undetected beneath her coat into school. She trained it to stand and look out from the pouch, with its forepaws perched on the rim. With its eyes peeping out at the alien world, with its curious nose twitching at smells. She taught it to sit on her shoulder, too – as she played her oboe or cycled her bike – crouched and clung to her dress. She left the cage door open at night so the hamster could come and climb up her sheet, scrabbling through covers and under her nightie to make its nest in her hair. It would run through her hands for exercise. It would sit on her head and cringe, like a rodent crown.

She had wanted a sheep, or a dog, or a goat, but her powers of persuasion had been in decline since clambering back from the cliff. She had been offered a hamster or some fish in a bowl. That was all she could choose. But the girl was grateful – truly grateful – and for the space of the next few weeks the hamster was all she could think of. She drew pictures of him; she sang him songs; she wrote homework both for and about him. She built him houses and runs and nests; she fed him, she washed him, she cleaned his cage; she cuddled him, groomed him, loved him dearly.

But even though he was vital and warm, she came to see he was like a toy. When not in his pouch, he lived in a box, in a cage, high up on a shelf. He wasn't wild, and he never had been. He hadn't known freedom, and though he might seek it, he would not have liked what he found. Flasher was more of a prisoner than she was; he was more of a Londoner than her or her parents. When the girl wasn't there, he would cower in his cage, he would run away and hide in his box at the merest hint of a noise. And, whilst a dog can grin and wag its tail, a cat can nuzzle and purr, Flasher was a wide-eyed, squiff-nosed fur-ball, with a furious beating heart which thumped beneath the cage of his ribs, as if about to explode. Poor Flasher! And though the girl was devoted to him, she knew that he wasn't enough.

It wasn't just pets she wanted now. It was all she felt she had been denied; all she had never experienced. Those days in the country had let her see so much more of what else was out there. Something crude and raw and proud. A pure and elemental life. Sky, and land, and sea. Forces more powerful and regal than people; laws that were crafted by nature. A simplicity, a strength, a solitude. A grandeur so absolute, so acute, it overwhelmed all other sense. But now she was here, in the heart of a city, with a tame caged rodent, a concrete earth, an electric dusk, a sliver of sky. And she knew she was living a lie.

She took desperate measures to feel alive. She refused to take baths: she waited for rain before running into the garden to wash. She ate with her fingers; she walked on all fours. For days she stopped speaking; she snarled.

Shortly after, her parents went out for the evening, leaving the girl with a friend. Before they had even sat down to eat, they received a message of panic. The girl was not in her bed; she was not in the house. Her last escape still fresh in their minds, her parents returned to their home. They searched through the rooms and found them all empty. There was no sign of her, no sign she was here. Yet the front door appeared to be locked from within. And the windows, too, were still locked. Finally, they went into the garden. They walked round the meagre fringe of the beds, and there they found her, under a bush, asleep on a bed of dry leaves.

Their first instinct was to bolt up the doors, to lock all the windows and keep them shut fast. To narrow her small world still more. To prevent her from doing what she thirsted to do because they believed that they cared for her welfare, because they believed it would help. But pity died in the face of that logic. They knew it couldn't be right. They had never wanted to limit her choices, to deny her the freedom to learn. They had only wanted to cherish and love her, to let her be happy, to allow her to live within what they and London could give.

But now both London and all within London were being destroyed by this child. The parents realised that all that they stood for, all that they knew – their home, their jobs, their interests, possessions – all which had seemed the essence of life – were despised and meant nothing to her. They meant nothing. Her parents felt that hollow of fear which has no expression beyond the dread that wrenches the gut and parches the throat, that separates madness from reason. They feared she hated all that they had; she hated them for the people they were, for the life they had chosen, for all that they stood for. Her will, her desire, was greater than theirs, and they knew they could not resist. They knew it was wrong for their love to be shown through constant constraints they imposed on the girl. They knew that the more they denied and obstructed, the more extreme her response.

They felt a terror they dared not name: a shame of no longer knowing their daughter; of knowing they couldn't persuade nor reason; of knowing no means by which they could please. She and they were such different beings, living in such dissimilar worlds, they couldn't relate nor comprehend. All they knew, instinctively, was that things as they were could not be sustained. There must be another solution.

The Farmhouse

The summer holidays approached. A time when London shrank in size, when carers seemed to go to ground; when parents drew on all they knew to help them through the long, hot days. And these two were the same. They didn't dislike the end of term, or having the girl in the house all day. What they disliked was the balance of time. Theirs too little, and hers too great. Days to fill that they could not fill. Whole weeks to occupy.

They sought their own parents for help. Those folk always willing, but never ideal – constrained by cities themselves. And it wasn't a city their daughter required. It was wilderness, and space, and freedom. Nothing less would tame her.

The more they considered the narrowing options, the more acute their daughter's needs, the clearer the answer became. Deep in the dark of maternal relations – remote and distant – they knew of a woman who lived on a farm. A woman not spoken to for years. A woman forgotten, lost in the past. But someone with the space and the time to offer all they were lacking. To give the girl what she wanted.

The woman sounded doubtful and cautious when they spoke to her on the phone. Wouldn't the girl get bored? The farm was secluded, far removed from the town. It was somewhere where nobody came. It was windy, and damp, and cold. There were large animals here; they were unused to children; they were capricious and could sometimes turn fierce. And, perhaps more important than anything else, there was nobody else on the farm.

The woman made clear she was busy by day. The girl would be left on her own for hours; she would have to fend for herself. Wouldn't she miss her life in London and want to be with her friends? The parents heard these false objections. These, they said, were all sound reasons – not deterrents – for her wanting to stay. Based on that, could she come for a week? Of course. If the girl was willing to be by herself, she was welcome to stay for as long as she liked. She could come whenever she wanted.

The drive to the farm was a perilous journey mute with foreboding and joy. The parents worried about their daughter, about the woman they barely knew, though they harboured a hope that time on the farm would leave its mark on the girl. It would leave her exhausted, contented, and full. It would make her reflect on their life in London; to see it refreshed through new eyes.

The girl's thought pattern strayed in a different direction. She sat in the car and stared before her, unwilling to close her eyes, or to blink, in case, on opening, she awoke to find the journey was only a dream. She sat, her body still and rigid, her mind alive and alert. She was willing the car away from London – from what London was, and all that was in it. She was willing it onwards towards the unknown; to a place where all that was known was the promise of something that London wasn't, or hadn't. Of something it never could be. Her mind was consumed by fantastical thoughts: that the week might extend and lead into two, and then to a year, to the end of her childhood, and then to the ending of time. They had told her nothing of where she was going. There were no stories to speak of, no pictures to see. She had never met this woman before. Yet she felt no fear in herself.

Dual carriageways led into busy main roads, and when these came to an end there were twisting lanes, snaking through fields and occasional towns. Then there was only a single track with hedges lining both sides. Hedges so high that they met at their crests, creating an archway, a shadowland. Grass grew down the spine of the track; and however slowly her father drove, the sides of the car were harassed and scratched by fingers of bramble and bush. When they met a car from the other direction, both skidded and shrieked to a halt. Then the other reversed to a bite in the hedge, and they edged a cautious way past.

From time to time the blindness of hedgerow was split by the gap of a gate. The girl would snatch a rush of blurred fields spinning confusedly past. Sudden raw smells arose from the land; there were squeals and cries, the flapping of wings; there was clanking, the suction of sinking wheels. Once or twice, they came to a rise, where over the top of the hedge they could see a valley laid out before them, entire. Everything caught in a snapshot of colour, then snatched back in a moment, extinguished.

The lanes went on without end. All seemingly similar, seeming the same. The girl had a sense she was moving in circles; she was spiralling out of the world that she knew; she was travelling not just through distance but time. She was moving through endless tiers of being. She and her parents were trapped forever – in a shadowy land, in a green-grey world, in a universe all of its own. In a place that was split by a blinding sun which wrapped an immense pure brilliance around them. They were caught up, caught by, and caught within it. Snared in delicious delirium; fused in an unfocused rush of white light.

At last they came to a wooden signpost leaning out from the hedge. They saw a track that led through an entrance – half concrete, half made of pebble and pothole – which crept up a slope and over a field to a blind stump of summit beyond. Then there, below them, stretched out a valley. And, halfway down the cantering hill, where the track dissolved into snatches of grass, was a small clutch of buildings which bordered a yard.

She knew the importance of first impressions. She knew the importance of making friends, from the very first moment they met. She knew that this woman – whoever she was – was her salvation, her hope. Without her acceptance she was back in the car in a week, in a day, in an hour. She knew all of this: she had tutored herself in what she would do and what she would say. Yet as soon as the car had come to a stop, she saw not the house nor the person beside it, she saw only a gate at the back of the yard, and beyond the gate was a field. All she could focus on was that gate. If she could reach it, if she could cling on, then she felt that she would be safe forever. They wouldn't be able to free her grasp; they wouldn't be able to prise her away. They would have no choice but allow her to stay. Filled with this all-possessing thought, she rushed from the car and ran through the yard till her arms were wrapped round the bars of the gate, and she found herself hugging its huge metal frame.

On the other side of the gate was a field, sloping away out of sight. It was a meadow, clothed with clumps of bright grass, with cowpats scattered like volcanic islands on a wind-torn, luminous sea. Beyond it, a tangle of sedge and reed cluttered and clouded the hazy distance. She tried to focus on what she saw, but it rose in a complex confusion of colour, confronting her senses and muddling her mind. She was overwhelmed by it all. Now all she could do was to lean on the gate, burying her head in the fold of her arms. Wind snatched at her hair and beat in her face in an infinite cycle of broken waves, till she felt her nose running and her eyes full of tears. And without knowing why, she felt somehow ashamed.

Hello.
Hello.
What are you looking at?
Nothing really. At the field.
Do you know what's in it?
I can't see anything.
At the bottom there. Out of sight. There's cows.
Cows?
Yes. There are nine cows, and they've all got names.
Do cows have names?
Why not? Cows aren't just things. They're all very different. They all have characters. Most are quite friendly. But there's one I can show you who's a real cow. She's nasty and mean and gorgeous.
Do you know all their names?
Of course. They're my cows.
Yours?
Yes. Do you like animals?
Yes.
That's lucky. We've got lots of animals here.
What have you got?
I've got dogs, cats, a pig, a horse, and those cows.
I've got a hamster.

Well, there we are. I don't like hamsters. I don't like chickens either.

Why not?

They're smelly, and messy, and a bit mixed up. They look silly, too.

Have you got any children?

No, I don't like children. I only like animals. You're all right though. Does it matter if there aren't any other children here?

No. It's fine. It's good.

Well, that's all right then. Do you want some tea?

Yes please.

I'm your aunt, by the way. Well, sort of your aunt.

In the kitchen, her parents were already seated at a large wooden table in the heart of the room. Flasher's cage was perched at one end. All the girl could see of the hamster inside was a frenzied nose and pink-white paws which protruded between the tight bars. Her bags and her oboe lay on the floor. The woman, her aunt, prepared the tea, handing the cups and plates to the girl, who laid them out round the table. Then she sat, as the adults started to speak about distant relations and distant events that inhabited long-distant worlds.

The girl let their words wash over her senses, switching her eyes to what lay in the room, seeing it coming to life. A black Labrador was trotting towards them. It had coy and mischievous eyes. She could tell at once it must be old by the grey on the underside of its jaw. It wagged its tired tail willingly, standing straight on rigid legs, inviting attention and hands. Eventually, it placed its head heavily on her mother's thigh, and looked at her with plaintive eyes, saying love me, love me, love me. Beside it was a younger dog, shivering unspent energy, jawing and panting at her parents' laps, snatching at the other's mouth, chasing into the hall and back, pacing the kitchen with a strange belly roll and a clip of nails on the floor. A tea-cosy cat sat aloof on a dresser, rounded and warm and perfectly still, surveying the turmoil with lazy eyes. It was wonderful, beautiful. All of it.

Tea was scones and jam, with a dollop of clotted cream spooned on the top. Milk came from a large metal pot in the fridge. It was thick, almost yellow; it was straight from the cows. She was told that the scones and the jam and the cream were all made here, they were made in this kitchen, they were made by this woman, her aunt.

The adults sat at one end of the table; they talked with the strained sense of certainty which comes from those who have rarely met, intrigued and yet so far removed from the world that was known to the others. Tea migrated to early supper – the parents resisting the secret truth of returning to London alone. The girl heard a snatch of their empty words as her fingers wove through the dogs' thick coats, as she felt the thrill of the touch. She glanced down at their watery mouths, at their honest sparkling smiling eyes, at their heads caught up in a pharaoh's roll of chequered tablecloth.

When the girl looked up at the windows again, she saw the colour was filtering away as light was washed from the sky. It was time for her parents to go. Her aunt was inviting her parents to stay, to remain in the clutch of the farm for the night. But London awaited; the journey was long. They knew that they needed to leave.

Her parents stood in the awkward courtyard, barged by the dogs as they jostled for affection. Now that the final moment had come, both mother and father seemed unwilling to leave and let the girl stay. They delayed their parting by making demands – insisting she wrote, insisting she phoned them – as if words alone could reach their daughter, or could change who she was, or could prise her away. As if they could tease her back to London; to coax her back into the car.

There could be no reprieve. They had to go. They knew she belonged here and they somewhere elsewhere. They kissed the girl; they hugged her tight. They promised to phone every day. Then they climbed in their car and drove up the track. In their mirrors they saw a slender figure watching them from a concrete island, surrounded by a sea of green, fading into the grey of the evening, till obscured by the crown of the hill. Then, in an instant, their daughter, the aunt, and the farm itself, were lost to their sight. They vanished.

The girl watched the car as it crept away, as it blurred with the curve of the blemished slope, till swallowed whole by the hill. A diminishing object so at odds with this world that was spread in its glory around her. Now there was only the swathe of the field cut by the cracked bone track – as bare as if her parent's car had never strayed from the road. The girl stood close to her aunt. She could feel her arm was wrapped round her shoulder, folding her into her dress. It was a firm embrace, like a squeeze. And, like everything else all around her – the animals, the grass, the bruising wind; the bushes, the tarnished sun, the sky – it felt the way that it ought to be. Much more than that. It felt right.

Why's your cat so big?

It's a country cat.

It's huge.

Yes. I shouldn't feed it really.

Won't it die if you don't feed it?

Most unlikely. There are rats in the barns. Voles in those banks. Birds in the hedges. Rabbits in the field. These cats may look dopey but they're killers.

There are rats?

Of course. Those are my other animals. Along with mice, toads, pigeons, snails and ducks, and all sorts. Only they aren't really mine. They just live here. Why don't I show you around, so you can see the animals I know? Then I'll leave you to find the ones that I don't.

In the softening light of the early evening the two started out on their tour. They walked past the kitchen door of the farm to a long, low building which mirrored the length of the yard. Its face was broken by five sturdy doors, each of which split in two.

The top half of the first door they came to was open and hooked back onto the wall. The girl stood on her toes to look in. Through the hollow, the almost fusty darkness, she could see the room had been partitioned by a low row of three steel bars. Beyond them, deep in the stagnant blackness, she could hear a grunting, a rustling of straw. Then the noise of something, bothered and heavy, struggling to get to its feet. Then no noise at all, but the sudden face of a coarse-haired, lollop-eared, beady-eyed pig on the other side of the bars. This huge white creature, splattered with mud, was a sow which answered to Rosie.

The top of the next door also stood open. From it, the neck and the head of a horse stretched proud as it watched them with lustreless eyes. Her aunt came forward and patted its neck; she signalled the girl to stay in the yard. Then she opened the lower half of the door, forcing the horse back into the stable, pushing it in on itself. The girl's eyes followed her aunt. She could see she was filling a metal basket which hung from a hook on the wall. She could see the horse, the shape of a horse, as a silhouette in the dusky room. She had never seen a creature so big standing so close to a human before.

The horse stood attentive, watching her aunt, in the same way as she was watching the beast. Just the same, with the same quiet curious interest, wanting to see what the woman would do. They stood so close they were almost touching. The horse's neck rose over her shoulder – its head above and in front of her aunt – so it had a clear view as it watched her working, filling the basket with hay. It wasn't like man and beast at all. It was like watching two people who know they are friends. Two friends who know each other so well that they don't need words to say what they feel. The girl could sense their intimacy: the horse's chin on the woman's shoulder, thanking her as she filled the basket, thanking her as she left.

Her aunt came out of the stable. She bolted the bottom half of the door.

Looking over her shoulder, the girl could see the horse's head as it re-emerged. She could feel its gentle gaze upon them, expressing a casual lazy interest, a disinterested love in its eyes.

That horse is huge.

Henry is quite big, you're right. He's a stallion.

Aren't you afraid of him?

No! He's a softie. He can bite though.

What was that huge thing hanging down?

Down from where?

From Henry.

His bridle?

No, not that. At the back.

His tail, silly. Don't you know what horses look like?

I meant the other thing – the thing coming out of his belly.

O that. That was his I'm-pleased-to-see-you.

His what?

His penis. His willy. His what-have-you.

Are they really that big?!

Sometimes. Not often. But they can get big. Henry does get excited sometimes.

They walked to the other side of the courtyard, to a split-level barn where her aunt informed her the cows were wintered and where they had calves. Beside it, she saw another courtyard, closed off from them by a gate. Beyond it, the red brick walls of a dairy. The walls were rift by two sliding doors, directly facing each other. One of them led from the shed to the courtyard, the other into the field. Inside, and running the length of one wall, the girl could see a feeding trough, and above it, hanging and shielded by beams, was a forest of tangled up tubes.

Next to the dairy stood the gate where the girl had clung when she first arrived. And next to the gate was a corner of farmhouse, completing the square of the courtyard.

39

The girl's aunt showed her the latch, explaining how to open the gate. Then they walked out into the field. In front of them, the land curled away to the foot of the valley. To their left was a tumult of green, overseen in the distance by a square church tower. To their right, beyond oceans of giddy grass, was the glass of a colourless sea. Behind them, at the near end of the farm, was a garden, half-hidden by sheltering hedge. To its side, set close to the wall of the stable, was a vegetable patch, a row of fruit bushes, an orchard where apples and plums and pears clung to the trees and shrugged off the wind.

This field they stood in belonged to her aunt. The field above it – beyond the farmhouse, split by the bald white track to the road – that belonged to her too. And a third smaller field behind the barns, where the cows were let out to graze.

The aunt presented it all to the girl with a careless sweep of her arm. The girl stared up at this new-found friend. Her hair was held in an untidy bun. Her dress was frayed and torn near its seam. Her arms were scratched, her cheeks were ruddy, her nails were broken and reddened with earth. The girl kept staring, she stared at this person – at this woman born only an hour ago – who lived in the midst of this beautiful chaos, this glorious, marvellous three-field world. Her aunt.

That night, the girl lay on her back in her bed, fiercely resisting the urge to sleep. She was working through the day in her mind, over and over again. The journey down, the courtyard, the kitchen, her aunt, the smell of the scones. The yawning fields, the grinning dogs; the horse, the pig and the cows. Then supper, bath-time, and bed.

Her bedroom stood beside the kitchen, on the ground floor, close to the farmhouse door. Lying still in the breathless dark, she could hear her aunt as she tidied up, as she shut the door and went upstairs. She could hear a noise from the kitchen still: the random yawn or scratch of a dog, curled by the Aga, chasing its dreams. She could picture the cat as it sat on a teapot, looking impassively into the room. She saw Rosie sat in a steaming bathtub, her hair in curlers, her trotters in bows. She saw Henry, becoming a huge fleshy penis, glancing at her with mischievous eyes. She saw her parents driving away, over the hill and into the distance, again and again, through the sun-spilt field. Always driving away.

The girl woke early. The sun had not yet broken free, and her room was gloomy and grey. She dressed swiftly, wanting to run in the fields before the house was awake. As she left her room, she glanced in the kitchen. She saw her aunt was already dressed; she was stood by the sideboard, her sleeves rolled up, as she doughtily kneaded a ball of dough. The dogs were also awake; licking their jaws and wagging their tails as they greedily shunted their bowls round the floor. The day had begun long ago. Not just in the house, but outside. She could see the stable doors were all open, the animals all groomed and fed.

By midday the farmhouse felt like her home, as if she had lived here forever. It was not that time grew somehow longer, but that each minute had grown more intense. There was so much being and doing around her. A curious blend of chaos and calm caught in a mesmeric whirl. Nothing she felt could be taken for granted, nothing she felt could be real. Though everything that was happening round her was so real, so live, so true.

41

In the days that followed, the girl discovered a different way to live life. It set in and stole her away. Each day, she rose around five in the morning for a cup of tea with her aunt. It was pleasant joining the older woman, but better still to be up before her, so she had the tea ready in time for her aunt, so she felt she had reason to be. They sat in silence, in the stealth of the half-light, feeling the warmth of the mugs in their hands, of the dogs that writhed round their knees. Feeling the greyness of day taking shape; feeling their skin come alive.

After tea, they went to the dairy. The girl stood in the doorway, not quite daring to enter. Intrigued by the cows and their pink, fleshy udders; by the tubes that her aunt had attached. The process seemed so awkward, so strange. Here was a leisurely row of cows eating hay from a stall on the wall, and there at the other end, milk. Glorious, frothy, creamy milk – rich and filling and thick.

After the milking the girl helped her aunt to shepherd the cows to the field. Then she ran across the waiting yard to give Rosie and Henry their feed. She liked to measure the meal for the pig, tipping the slops out into a bucket, mixing the strange concoction around with dregs of the last day's milk. She liked to pour it into the feeder, watching Rosie attacking her dish, watching her look of cross-eyed confusion at the slops which stuck to her snout. Then they went to Henry, who her aunt fed herself – though the girl was allowed to offer a carrot, extended on the flat of her palm. She could feel his long and pointed tongue washing over her skin; its muscular power as it searched her fingers, scratching them, scouring them clean. It was only when all the creatures were fed that they sat down to breakfast themselves.

After their meal they were out again – clearing, and cleaning, and brushing, and washing. And by then, perhaps, it was nine o'clock, with a full day open before them. For the rest of the morning, her aunt would be busy – chasing down chores in the fields or in town, returning only at lunch. Then again, she was gone in the afternoon: she was riding Henry, she was walking the dogs, she was mending a fence in her fields. Not till evening did they come together for a further round of feeding and grooming, of closing and putting away. Then they sat exhausted in the kitchen for supper, before locking the doors and going to bed.

Almost all of the day was left to the girl; she had the time to herself. Her aunt was too busy to break her routine, though at first she seemed conscious the girl was alone and thought to amuse her by setting her chores. She asked her to pick all the raspberries and currants; she asked her to brush out the top of the barn; she asked her to sort out the feed. The girl was keen to oblige. She could anticipate tasks without being told; she seemed to know what had to be done. And between these tasks, she diverted herself. She was never idle nor dull. And when her aunt saw the girl wasn't bored – that she was content to do as she liked – she ceased her demands and let the girl be. An unspoken bond of trust grew between them – the aunt respecting the girl's independence, the girl determined to win that respect.

This was a solitude new to the girl. A being on one's own which was so not alone that the girl felt no absence or longing. Within what was, what already existed, a universe was standing entire. All she needed to do was explore it.

For the first few days she stayed close to the farm, exploring the outhouses, watching the animals, discovering the orchard and fields. Just behind the dairy, close to the gate, was a Judas tree that stood on its own. It was broad and thick with a mantle of leaves, though stooped by the challenging wind. It rose above the line of the buildings, giving full sight of the yard. This became her vantage point, her crow's nest onto the world. It was where she began in the early morning; it was how she ended each day. It was where she would go when torn for choice by the dozen adventures she wanted to have – all of them – all in that moment. It was where she would be when she felt in her bones that the farm was calling to her. It was what she would climb when she felt the need to stand guard and protect her magical world, to capture it all in a single glance, to reassure herself it still there. At such times, she would clamber into the branches until obscured by the green-yellow leaves, and from there she would look – she would listen and wait – finding a peace in what lay before her, finding a haven inside.

During the day, she would make her rounds. These were not the same as her aunt's: they were her secret, personal chores. She went through the house, inspecting each room. She released the wasps that were trapped behind windows; she rescued beetles from shelves; she found new homes for snails in the peelings; she helped spiders caught in the bath. She went through each of the rooms downstairs, where she knew her aunt had laid snares. On her third day she found a terrified mouse marooned in a plastic trap. She tipped it into her wanting hands and carried it round to the side of the farmhouse, releasing it into the fields.

The following day she found a bird, brought in by chance or by one of the cats. The bird was lying in shock on the floor, and she thought to scoop it up in her hands. At the first faint touch the creature panicked, flapping frantically round the room, dashing itself against the walls, till it fell in exhaustion onto the floor. Then, stunned, the girl was able to lift it up, to carry it out and into the field, to speak calm words as she set it down, to keep vigil till it fluttered away. Later that day, another bird, though this one seemed too crippled to fly. One wing hung limp, though perfectly soft, and flesh was torn from its side. The girl knew that the bird was unable to fly. She caught it up in her cradling hands, she took it outside and into the yard, and from there to a boulder which stood to one side. She laid the broken bird on her altar; she picked up a half-brick and smashed its skull.

Once the girl had inspected the house, she explored the stables and barns. Here there were fatal traps and poisons, unlike those in the house that were safe. Here, in the space of her first few days, she found two mice and three rats. Some were still in the throes of death: scrabbling, vomiting, wild-eyed, and ruptured. She watched them minutely; she stroked them for pity; she waited beside them until they were dead.

She found an assortment of other creatures that had fallen the victim of cats. A rabbit, desperately clawing the yard, its backbone crushed and its hind legs useless, staring at death from its hollow eyes. A barn owl that was missing an ear; a bat whose wings had been shredded. So many things. And so beautiful. If still alive, she shattered their skulls. If dead, she laid them out in a line, in a low stiff row by her killing stone.

Between the tool shed and the farmhouse was a narrow sliver of land. It was suitably close to the gardening tools, and close to the shelter of trees. It was shady, and out of the wind. It was here that the girl chose a patch for her graveyard. She buried the animals separately, each with a flat stone placed on their bodies so they couldn't be dug up by foxes. She made crosses with twigs to mark each of the graves. She planted a border of flowers round the plot. It became like a garden to her.

Into this garden her aunt came to see her after one week of her stay. She came to ask if the girl had got bored, if she thought it was time to go home. Without looking up, the girl replied that she wished to stay on – here in the farmhouse – that she wanted to stay here forever. Her aunt left the girl to tend her flowers, to mark her infant graves with headstones. A short while later she returned. She told the girl she had called her mother, and her mother had said she could stay. The words were spoken; the decision made. There was nothing else she need say.

Once more alone in her crowded garden, the girl buried London alongside the bodies. She buried it deep and placed stones upon it. She forgot that ever it was.

Now, with the endless summer before her, the girl extended her bounds. She skirted the full extent of the farm to see what was lying beyond. To the north, was the road. To the east, a field. To the west, again, a patchwork of fields. Though beyond the next and the next were some dunes, and down from the dunes was the sea. To the south, the field dipped into a valley. At its foot was a snarl of deep undergrowth which clung to a bank beyond a wire fence, then slipped to a riverbed hidden by reeds.

At its mouth, the reedbed was solid and thick as it met with the startled and spiny grass of the dune protecting the sea. At its tail, the bed was engulfed by the land, growing weaker and distant and petering out.

At daybreak the valley was shrouded in mist – the bushes ghosted a damp cold silver, the reedbed shivering grey. As morning grew, it seemed to sweat under the eye of the piercing sun. It sighed and swooned in the heat of the day. But the bed was never at rest. Neither silent nor still. There was always a sound of vibrant birdsong; there was always a shocked and shivering lament that writhed and rose from the tangle of stems.

Between the field and the hidden waters, a wire fence ran the length of the valley, without a stile or a gate. The girl stood small within its tall shadow, warily tracing its route through the grass, wondering why it was what it was, and how it came to be here. She looked to the reeds as if they could speak. She wanted to know if the fence was designed to shut things in, or to shut them out. She wanted to know why this place existed – so separate, so distant, so lost.

For her, the farm was full of her friends, but here was a solitude matching her own. Now she had seen the golden reeds, she was lured to them like a moth. Here, she felt, was a home of her own. A place in which she could lose who she was. Here, she felt, she would find.

The girl was sure she could scale the fence, yet she felt unwilling to try. Perhaps she would break the trust that had grown, which bonded her to her aunt. Perhaps her reluctance was deeper still. Something locked in her innermost being, for which she couldn't find words.

She stared at the fence which stood before her; she stared at the swirling body of reeds, at the absence of anything lying beyond the tensioned lattice of wire. She was looking into another world – a world so far removed from all others – beyond comprehension, beyond her control.

Even before she crossed the fence, the reeds became her guilty secret, the single thing she felt unwilling to speak about to her aunt. This feeling persisted; it grew stronger through time. Yet it did not stop her from crossing the wire. The girl was not afraid of fear. She knew the depths of solitude. If they were all that sheltered here, then she could make them her friends. She could dispel the nagging voice that said what she did was surely forbidden. She could quell the insistent foreboding that washed like a poison around her veins.

The girl stood studying the fence. It was sturdy and strong, with large wooden posts every ten or twelve feet, driven into the earth. The bottom four foot of the fence was wire mesh, buried into the ground. Above it, three rows of tortuous barb, twisted together so they couldn't bend. The structure was built so as not to be breached. No bushes stood overlooking the line, allowing her to climb and leap over. She would have to burrow beneath.

There were dense clumps of knotted grass that grew against the base of the fence. She pulled at one to test its strength, finding it come away in her hand. And with it a thick clutch of earth. Encouraged, she followed the line of the fence, moving farther away from the farm, choosing a spot not far from bushes that shadowed her from the world. She knelt; she tugged at a fistful of field.

The grass like hair, the earth a face, she held its head in her grasp. And now, with six shocked heads in a row, she had forged a crude and shallow trench, deep enough she could slither through. She twisted into the earth on her belly, feeling the scratching wire on her back, wriggling through until clear. Then she reached between the strangle of wire, clutching the dying heads in her hands, patting them back into place and concealing her trench.

She looked through the fence, up the slope of the field. All she could see of the farm was its roof, and the distant crown of the Judas tree. So far removed, and so distant. Even the field, her familiar field, where the cows were contentedly wandering and grazing, seemed remote, and lost beyond reach. This place she had entered was somehow different. Another world. An alien world. A wilderness. An oblivion. A place where people did not go, or could not go, or dared not. Or if they went, they didn't return. Not as the people they were.

She shrugged off her imaginings to inspect the place she had found. In front of her, a gradual bank slid softly into the wreathes of reed. She could hear the lisp of the secret water lapping against their whispering stems, though blind to their tangled world. The reeds stood tall and proud above her, their deep dense body dark and cold. Impenetrable, immense. Yielding no way in nor through. The only path was a meagre trail, crushed in the earth at the foot of the bank, between the fence and the reed.

The girl set out along the track, stumbling and staggering over the scrub, her steps inclined to the sea. Rounding a corner, she spied a house. So unexpected, she flinched. As if someone had crept up and breathed on her neck.

She stepped back, to look at it closely. It was a house, or had been a house at one time. Though now it seemed the shell of a home. It had a chimney, and most of four walls, two of which once had had windows. And there was a space on one side for a door. But that was all that there was. It had no roof, no glass in the windows, no fixtures inside, no features, no beams. It was sunk and engulfed and surrounded by brambles; it was being consumed from outside and within. Straining to look through one of the windows, she could see the shape of a single room, scarred and part-buried by scrub. The inside was woven with nettles and weed, as though the house had sprung from the land, and was now reverting to earth.

The next day she came to the ruin again, with a sickle she stole from the shed. She cut a narrow path to the door, and then another into its heart so she could reach to the walls. The ruin was built of layers of slate, compressed and wedged beneath its own weight, defending it from the wind. But time had worn its body down, eroding its sides till only one seemed safe enough to be scaled. She hacked her way towards it. Then she dropped the sickle and pulled herself up the slippery side of the slate, till she had clawed her way to the summit. She sat down and surveyed her new world.

In front of her was a sea of reeds – a restless, formless, cantankerous mass. Behind her, the sanctuary of the farm, where her aunt and her animals waited for her, greedy to smother her whole in their love. And here, in between those two separate worlds, was a second crow's nest, a second retreat. Where she could come when loneliness beckoned – when she needed the space to be alone – to drink her solitude dry.

From then on, the ruin became her world. She went as soon as her rounds were done. Or, if she found it was calling her early, she forgot her rounds and went straight there. She spun down the field, she snuck through her trench, she slid down the bank and along the path, she scratched through the brambles and scaled the wall. And then, there she was – in splendid seclusion – looking out over the reeds. She was there in her ruin before she awoke. She was there before she was even aware her footsteps had taken her there.

The girl looked out on the reeds. They were so twisted and fraught, and the cry that they made was so utterly cold, that though she felt compelled to stay she could barely endure to witness their pain. To see their torment being laid bare, their agony being exposed. She tried taking Flasher for company. But as soon as he heard the reeds' lament, as soon as he saw their frenzied surge, he panicked, terrified. The girl had to press him into his pouch as he squirmed and strove to plunge from the wall. She could feel him scratching and biting her palm. She was forced to take him back to the farm.

Having no one else, wanting no one else, she took her oboe down to the reeds. Ever since she arrived it had sat in its case, unpractised, neglected, and gathering dust. But now she thought it might be her friend, it might serve as a guide, perhaps as a shield, in the swirling sea of unknown. She sat on the wall and took up the oboe, slotting her reed in its bore. For a while she was silent, listening intently to the endless army of chattering reeds. Listening to the music they spoke. Then she raised the oboe to her lips. She tried to mimic their speech.

The reeds shuddered and gasped, confused for an instant. Then they hissed their urgent reply. Again, the girl cried back to them, piping and speaking the same brittle notes, rasping and shrill as she sought to be heard.

The reeds didn't understand what she said. Or, if they did, they failed to acknowledge the greetings she puffed out towards them. They had moved on already to other secrets, to other riddles they had to impart. They screamed their ghostly music at her; they shivered their sorrow and anguish.

The oboe repeated her urgent truths. I am your friend. I want to know you. I want to know who you are. I want to know why you have chosen to live here. Tell me. Let me enter your world.

As a body, the reeds thrashed back at her boldness, jeering an answer that broke in her face like the rasping of thunder, the crashing of waves. Awesome and ugly, and empty of sense.

Undaunted, she tried once again. Talk to me. Speak to me slowly, please, so I can understand what you say. The girl blew her heart through the single reed, as though it might translate her longing to those which lay in their oily bed; as though it could filter reply. A million ecstatic voices warring; desperate their nonsense be heard.

If they spoke, they were speaking a different language – a language that she must learn too. Placing the oboe down on the wall, she approached the riotous reeds. Cautiously, she edged towards them, feeling curious but also afraid. As if approaching an untamed beast, a creature of immeasurable strength, uncertain of what they might do.

She shuffled down the neck of the bank, extending both of her arms before her. She reached for the nearest reed. She shut her eyes as she grasped the stalk, as she felt her fingers closing upon it, unsure of what the reaction might be. In her mind she could see the whole bed of reeds joining as one and rising against her, dragging her in and drowning her deep in the waters in which they were pitched.

She tugged. She tugged again. The reed resisted. Its neighbours seemed to come alive, frantic to save their sibling in peril. They swirled and scratched against the fist which was clutched around the single stem. All about her, all around, the basin of reed assumed one voice, singing a stinging hymn of hate.

Don't pluck me! Don't!

She pulled again. And this time the reed gave way in her hand. It broke in half, at its stem. The girl fell backwards onto the bank. She clawed her way towards the ruin – still on all fours, her back to the ground – her eyes transfixed on the stern belt of reeds, on the one blind stump she had savaged.

Back on the wall, she examined her prize – the four feet of dying reed in her hand. At its tip was the lavish head of its seeds, like the flame of a candle, the wing of a bird outstretched and ready to fly. Beneath it, a series of long thin leaves: coarse, dark-green, and sharp to the touch. Those at the top were closely spaced, all pointed upward, and fresh. Those beneath were born of bruised knuckles; they were hardier, older and torn. The stem itself had a sheath of leaf which shed in her hand like the skin of a snake, revealing a clean, white bone.

The girl felt sure this reed could speak. She knew that it knew their mystical language; she knew it could summon their words. She twisted its stem and splintered its sinews, sizing two pieces down for her oboe. She pulled a loose thread that hung from her dress, binding both stems side by side. Then she slipped the sound-piece into the bore in place of the one that was there. She blew.

Nothing.

How could there be nothing? How could it be so? Here, where everything had a voice, how was it right she was mute? How could she hear, without being heard? How could she fail to be understood? All around was a tumult of sound, and all could speak except her. As an outcast she listened, angry, ashamed; hearing the pulsing music of life which burgeoned amidst the blistered reeds.

Through the stealthy spine of their long bending stems, she could hear a constant chatter of birds. Of so many birds. One was a song that began with a shriek, then a startled pause, then a series of notes, sung in a voice which was fluty and thin. Changing the living reed for her own, she piped out the same fiery sound. She listened; then she heard it returned. She piped it out once again. She paused, awaiting reply. Instead, another song began: a high-pitched trill like a fishing reel being wound round at great speed. The oboe struggled to copy the sound. But now she was drawn to a different noise that rang like a cymbal struck at the sky. *Ching*, her oboe replied. *Ching*.

Two circling crows interrupted their flight to perch for a while on her chimney. She supposed they were drawn by her sounds. So she played them more of her wild wind music, charming the birds with her song.

Here, in the ruin, she felt she was safe. From here she felt she could go and explore the restless world that was laid out around in the knowledge of easy retreat. When she was ready, she set down her oboe, she climbed from her wall and pushed through the nettles, she scuffed down the track to the sea. Though only the distance of three short fields, the margin below the fence was dense with rills and potholes that slowed her progress, with pockets of long spiny sedge. Above her, low branches stretched wayward fingers, clawing and scratching her hair.

Here, at the border between two fields, was an earth-hedge, covered with bramble and thorn. It ran from the top of the slope through the grass, stopping just short of the fence. In the farther field, a clutch of crows was waddling through the clumpy grass, practising their low flight. Their feathers havocked by gusting wind, their fanned wings flayed by the breeze. Beyond the shelter of the reeds, the girl could see a rising squall savaging the knoll of the dune, pressing its breath on the land.

Another earth-hedge rose beside her as she came to the final field. Now she could taste the sea on her lips. She could feel the strengthening wind. The reeds knew it too – they grew tighter here, spitting a fiercer song through their teeth, bowing in greater homage and pain. She spun through a hollow – a rich patch of green – then stepped up a rise and into the dune. She scrambled on her hands and her knees, pulling herself up its wall. As she reached its summit, a bald rush of wind struck out and snatched at her face. So strong it felt an invisible hand was grasping her body and dragging her back. She clung to the grass to steady herself, smudging the tears from her eyes.

The fence that had been to her side all the while had sunk itself into the sand. From here there was only a thick belt of dune to separate man from the reeds. Before her, the steep sandy hill slid forwards, onto a beach swept clean by the wind. And beyond the beach – stretched over the globe, stretched over its skin to the endless horizon – was an immense, cold, guttural sea.

Is it safe to swim in the sea?
Certainly. And this is the best time of year. It's warm.
Do you think I can go?
Of course.
When?
Whenever you like.
When are you free?
Me? I don't want to swim. I haven't swum for years.
But when can you take me?
Why should I take you? Go by yourself.
To the sea?
Yes. It's over there. Look.
Can I go? On my own?
Why ever not? Nobody's going to assault you on the way. All the same, there are one or two rules. You must tell me when you're going. And only swim between the red buoys. Obviously, don't go swimming when it's rough. And don't go out beyond your depth.
Beyond my depth?
The beach is sandy and very flat. You can walk out twenty yards and still be in your depth. But beyond that the current is strong. If you think you're drowning, then wave and shout. Someone will probably hear you. And take a towel. There's a sort of footpath just above the ley.

Above the what?

The ley.

What's the ley?

That place down there. The thing in the valley covered by reeds.

What is it?

It's a ley. I don't know what they do, they just are.

What happens in them?

Nothing. Birds and animals live there. And there's water underneath the reeds, so it's a dangerous place to visit. It's fenced off anyway. The path runs just this side of the fence. There are gaps in the hedges between the fields. Then there's a dune, and you're there. Early morning's the best time to go. Once we've done the feeds. I used to swim in the sea every day when I was younger, you know.

The girl set out at dawn next day, following the route her aunt had suggested. It was easier to walk through the field. The path she trod was more even and open. She strode along beside the ley, just paces from where she had stumbled before. She slipped through the gaps between the fence and the hedges; she clambered onto the dune. From here, she found a path through the sand.

The girl was wearing a dressing gown, with a towel she had slung round her neck. The wind was lame. The reeds in the ley sighed breathlessly, cloaked in the eery strands of a mist that muddied the early morning. The beach lay raw and deserted before her, basking in its sheer beauty.

Ten feet from the sea she slipped off her robe, discarding her towel and her shoes. The sand beneath her toes was soft; the tide was ebbing and low. She gasped as her naked ankles met with the cold embrace of the waves.

She shuffled forwards, now knee-deep, standing on the tips of her toes as the chill waves rose to greet her. She waded up to her waist. An intense fold of coldness closed round her legs; it crept round her belly, her arms.

The girl plunged, and swiftly resurfaced. She stood tall, catching her breath. Then another plunge. And this time, on purpose, she kept her knees bent so only her head reemerged. She counted to thirty – evenly, slowly – her body mirroring the fluid motion, the rise and fall of the constant waves, as they rolled beyond her and lapped at the beach. Then she pushed off with her toes and raised her legs, swimming a parallel line to the dune till she reached the mark of the last red buoy.

She stopped and stood, glad to find she was still in her depth. The sea felt warmer now. Her body felt warm. She knew out there in the open air the wind would cut through her skin. But here it was luxurious and calm – being washed and stroked by the joyous water, cleansed by its healing salt. She felt no suction, no drag from the waves. Instead, a murmur, a caress. She was held in a palm of infinite strength which invited her to lay back her head, to cease all motion, to close her eyes. Whatever she did, however she lay, the sea matched her shape and altered its own, becoming her living cast. Every fraction of water, every fraction of her, met perfectly and without any effort – bound in an absolute kiss, an absolute fit.

When she came out of the water the breeze iced against her, slicing through to her bone. Hurriedly, she dried and got dressed. Then, to lessen the pain, she ran. She ran looking downwards to kill the distance. Down as she slip-slid over the dune; down as she sped through the grass.

Her eyes were clouded with blinding tears; the rising wind at her back. She looked askance as she came to a hedge, then – after a discord of time – to the next. She cut diagonally up through the field, over the rise that led to the gate.

And there, at the fringe of her haste-hidden sight, a cow raised its head in surprise as she fled. It stood watching her till she was home.

She changed and dried in her room. It was wonderful feeling this warm again. She dressed and came out to the yard. Out and into the sweating sun. She felt cleansed, and so, so alive. For the first time, she felt truly awake. She could feel herself breathing; the pulse of her blood as it flowed through her body; her taut muscles, the stretch of her skin. She saw everything keenly, as if the sea had washed cataracts from her eyes. Her ears caught the sound of a mouse's footfall; the sigh of a flower; the motion of clouds. She could smell the scent of the world around her; she could taste its life on her tongue. She was part of it all; bound up in it all. She and it were as one.

Each day from then on, she went swimming. This was a whole new way of being; a whole new way to live life. Now, she skipped the morning rounds. She rolled out of bed and went straight to the beach. The less awake the better it was – the better it was to be kissed awake by the gentle caress of the sea. To lie in its cradle, and there to awaken. There to awake, to be born. By the time she came out of the body of water, she was vital, acutely alive. Trembling with energy; electrically charged; urgent to live the new day. This feeling, this being consumed her so fiercely she could focus on nothing beyond.

It was only after a fifth day of swimming, a fifth giddy dash back over the fields, as she was passing close to the ley, that she lifted her head, she stopped and listened. It was only then that she was she aware – and only then, for the very first time – that she was not on her own.

The Beast

The girl stopped and listened.

Over the crush of the reeds, the slice of the wind, the murmur of water, she could hear something else was in motion. Somewhere, beyond the line of the fence, down the bank, in the hidden strangle of bush. There was something moving around. She switched her eyes towards the noise. She could hear it without being able to see. It was somewhere below her, low, out of sight. It wasn't a heavy or laboured sound, but more than a rabbit or fox would make. More than any creature she knew. It was a moving, a busying, that kept its own time, out of pace with the natural music that swamped the fringe of the ley. Yet the girl did not think it a threatening sound. Nor did she think the creature could know she was standing there, and so close. She wanted the beast to show itself; she wanted the wind to drop for a moment, for the reeds to cease their idle commotion, so she could hear it more clearly.

She started forward as if to explore, but an urge of caution restrained her. She was in a bathrobe, cold and wet, and like this she couldn't enter the ley. She strained her ears to absorb the sound, to convince herself it was real. Yes, there it was: it was purposeful, intent. Then she walked away slowly, still watching the bank – fixedly watching that blind patch of scrub from where she had first heard the curious noise – only turning and breaking into a run when she felt she was quite out of sight.

Had she been anyone else, she might have forgotten what she had heard. But the girl couldn't let such things pass.

Equally, she was far too proud to ask her aunt if she knew. The sound was clearly coming from something – that something was down there to make it. And since that was so, she would find it herself. There was nothing she knew of that frightened her.

In the hours that followed, her mind was a mine of conjecture and fancy. She had thought that the ley was cut off and deserted, it was starved of life except for the marsh birds. But clearly, that wasn't so. There was something else – at least one other – that lurked unseen in its depths. Was this a creature trapped in the ley – held there on purpose, against its will? Was that why the ley was fenced off? Was that why her aunt had told of its dangers? Was that what made the reeds cry? The girl slapped back her idle notions. She knew such whims were a weakness. She would rather face her doubt than just dream it. She told herself that things were benign, and generally they proved to be so. She had no reason to be suspicious; only reason to search for the truth.

She dressed and had breakfast. Then she borrowed her aunt's binoculars and slipped down the field to the ley. She slithered cautiously under the fence, looking about her with care. She crept stealthily up to the ruined house. Once on its walls, she felt safe. This was her space, her sanctuary. It was high up, beyond the reach of another, with a clear view that stretched in all directions. Training the binoculars first on the dune, she began a systematic sweep, looking for something unknown.

All day she looked out onto the ley. She explored each crevice, each undulation; each shifting shadow, each pocket of breeze that might transmute into life.

Nothing unusual caught her eye. She felt both relieved and dismayed. Knowing something was there, she wanted to see it. To confirm to herself it was there. She knew it was there; she had heard it moving; though she could almost convince herself that it might have been a trick of her mind. It might have been something so small and so slight, something so trivial as to lack any meaning, that she wouldn't hear it again.

As the hours wore on, she told herself she was willing to share this space with another. However much she thought it her own, she could let other creatures into the ley. She believed in the right to coexist, in the harmony of all that existed. She and the thing could continue to be. If their paths crossed, they would deal with it then. That was what animals did. She climbed gratefully down from her perch on the wall, a benevolence flooding her senses.

She left the track at her usual place to squirm through her trench leading under the fence. As her head and shoulders were wriggling through, she heard the noise once again. There, from somewhere behind her.

An irrational panic seized her mind. She pulled her body through in such haste that she tore a hole in her dress. She turned her head to follow the sound, her eyes like an animal's caught in a trap. Under a bush and dancing away was the fluffy tail of a rabbit. She could tell it was equally scared. The girl tugged the grass in dismay at her weakness. There could be no kindness, no coexistence – not till she knew what the creature was.

The next morning, the girl went swimming again, walking tentatively through the field. Her eyes forever upon the reedbed: transfixed by the bushes which stood to its side.

As she came to the first earth-hedge, she slackened her steps, she came to a stop. She could hear the same noise again. Behind the bushes, and clearer now. The sound becoming distinct.

Something large was moving swiftly: it was skurrying along the base of the bank. She could hear its feet in the dew-wet grass; she could hear a noise like the parting of reeds. Then a heavier sigh as the creature touched them, as it seemed to clatter inside. It was such a precise, such a singular sound – so clearly not the sound of the ley – she found it hard to believe she had never consciously heard it before. Then, as abruptly as it had begun, there was silence. A silence so long that she knew that the creature was no longer there. It had been absorbed. It had gone.

The girl resumed her walk down the path, over the dune and onto the beach.

Her swim did not satisfy her. It was cold; her body refused to be warmed. She tried to lie her head in the waves, but instead of being cocooned in their calm, it seemed as though she was falling through them, and she needed to thrash to keep floating. She didn't feel at one with the sea. She felt intrusive, ridiculous. Before long, she came out and dried. Then she started back home.

All the way along the fence she was listening, hoping the sound would emerge. All the way she heard nothing. Nothing that shouldn't be there. Only once or twice, perhaps, she could hear a muffled yawn of the reeds in the distance. Nothing more, yet so much. She knew the beast was disrupting her flow; defiling her innocent joy of the ley; spoiling the pleasure she took of the sea. And, like the sea, it wore her down. Imperceptibly, irreversibly.

After breakfast she went to the shed. She selected a spade and a stretch of sacking; she dragged them down the slope of the field till she reached the line of the nearest hedge. Here she rested in semi-shadow, feeling the day unfolding around her. Seeing the sun ease over the ley, seeing the hue of the reeds growing richer, seeing the mist being burnt from their feathers, seeing their swathes being burnished in red and then being gilded in gold. She was watching and listening to the sharpening morning. Here, right here, in the very place where she had heard that unknown noise scarcely more than an hour ago. Though now, she could only hear the ley – only the restless breath of the reeds, huge to her ear, yet familiar. So known to her in its intricate shades that she knew there was no other noise.

Convincing herself that she was alone, the girl climbed up the neck of the mound and prodded its growth with her shoes. Finding a tender spot in its skin, she raised the spade above her head, then brought it forcefully down – time and again – as if slicing into a giant hedge-snake which lay the full length of the field. She set the spade to one side, then got down on her knees to bundle out its entrails using her hands. Grass, thorn, bramble, root, earth, tumbled down the side of the hedge. When the girl had removed as much as was loose, she took up the spade once again. Again, she stabbed at the hedge's head; again, she knelt to scoop out its brains. She worked without ceasing, until she had carved a natural hollow in which she could hide. It was a foot in depth, a foot in width, and almost a full four feet long. A shallow grave. Then she placed the sacking over her nest; she slipped off the hedge and returned to the farm.

Her hands were wounded and raw. She washed them thoroughly, as though cleansing a sin, then she joined her aunt in the kitchen for lunch. She didn't return to her refuge at once. She sensed that this creature, like so many beasts, would only appear at the margins of day, when the sun was spent and had lost its fury, when the fading colours preceding the dusk would shield it, affording it sanctuary. The girl sat unmoved on the crown of the gate, counting out time as she watched her aunt laying out feed in the dairy. Only once all the cows had been milked did the girl leave the farm and dance down the field, before clambering onto the hedge. Then she lay in the trench, beneath the loose sacking, waiting for something unknown.

From where she lay, the fence stood before her, scarcely six feet away. On its farther side was a patch of green, a slip of bank, the crouching outlines of broken bushes, the fierce sharp fingers of scrub. And beyond them, the dense bent heads of the reeds. She propped up the front of the sacking with twigs, creating a thin slit through which she could see. Then she lay on her stomach, her elbows grounded, her chin in her hands as she watched.

The day declined by degrees. The reeds ceased sweating, and their restless chant faded into an undertone with the lessening of the wearying wind. Colours grew deeper, objects opaque. Birds flew in from the fields and the sea, darting above the crested reeds, plucking their food from the air. The earth seemed to settle, it seemed to exhale, feeling the weight of the day.

The girl didn't know what she waited for, or what it was she might see. She didn't know if it was going to come.

She didn't know what she would do if it came. She didn't know if it was friendly or hostile. If she would be tempted to run towards it, or to turn and flee up the field. She had brought nothing with her to use to defend her. Despite this, she wasn't afraid. She felt she was safe on the massive earth-hedge, beyond the reach of those in the field. And she was here, on this side of the fence, while the creature lived on the other. She wasn't nervous, nor was she impatient. She knew in her heart it would come.

It began with the slightest of rustling. At first she thought the fragile sound was no more than the wind in the grass. It was coming in from the sea and the dune, coming towards her, becoming louder – though still so faint she was scarcely persuaded she was able to hear it at all.

Though now there could be no mistake.

The creature was moving with speed and with care close by the fringe of the reed. She could hear the grass as it gave way beneath it, moving aside as the legs brushed through it. She could even hear the footfall itself, as it squashed alongside the margins.

The creature was down at the foot of the reeds. So close to their stems it was almost within them. Then, as it came up closer to her, she could hear the sound of its breath. She could hear that its breathing was flighty and shallow; it was unnaturally thin for a beast of its size. She peered out from under her hide. Though high on the hedge, she couldn't quite see to the base of the bank where it trod. She could only hear it, she could only sense it, moving with speed and with stealth.

Then she heard the snap of a twig underfoot.

Only then did she gauge how softly it moved; how easily it crossed the terrain. Only then did she gauge how close it had come; how close it was to her still. Then, as swiftly as it had approached, it slipped away into silence. Seeming to be dissolved in the air, melted into the reeds.

The girl waited. She thought it was certain to reappear somewhere farther beyond. Or, if not, to retrace its steps to the beach. Or perhaps to climb up onto the bank. It would come towards this stretch of the fence to scale the wire and confront her. It was going to reveal what it was.

But it did none of these.

The girl waited. Time dripped invisibly; it chased away from the shrunken world where she lay. She thought the creature must be resting, it must have fallen asleep. Right here, at the foot of the fence. She listened for breathing. For half an hour she waited, breathless. Then, unable to wait any more, she crept from her lair and went up to the fence. She stood on tiptoe and looked down the bank.

There was nothing there.

The next morning was overcast, and cool. The mist was slow in wanting to rise, and the sun too thin to thaw its shroud. The girl sat on the wall in her ruin, looking blindly down at the reeds. She felt that only by getting closer could she learn what sort of a creature this was. The beast was everywhere and nowhere. It was a part of the ley; it lived within it. But, when it chose, it could disappear. It could blend within the reeds and be gone. It was always, always just out of reach. She felt that they both had to be in the ley before she could see it alive.

An unexpected noise disturbed her. She looked up, attempting to trace the sound. Beside the margin of the reeds, she caught sight of a shadow approaching fast. The girl slipped down behind the wall; she crouched on a slate shelf carved in the ruin, which jutted over the crest of the thorn. She knew what it was that approached. She knew, though she had never heard it before – never this close to the ruin. She wondered why it was out so late, then guessed that the mist and the softened air had tempted it into extending its hunt.

Now she was blind. She was trapped in her ruin. She felt she had an advantage of height, and also perhaps of surprise. But that was all. She squashed her body into the corner, as if wanting to blend with the wall. She felt foolish, and so, so exposed. To be found out, standing here on a shelf, would be demeaning, it would be unfair. But the humiliation would bring with it knowledge. And she wanted to know what the creature was. More than all, she wanted to know.

She listened intently. Yes, she could hear it. The creature had come down the track. Now it must be standing, unmoving, right by the side of the reeds. There was a pause. Then she heard brisk movement – a scatter of footfall – coming directly towards her. Then, once again, it stopped. Just on the other side of the wall. And now it was sufficiently close that she could hear the sound of its breath. She could almost feel the warmth of its body, its pulse, its beating heart. She sensed the creature was at one with the ley. It knew every bush, every roll of the bank. This was its home, where it felt most at home. It was confident, unhurried, and sure. It was part of the ley, and part master of it. A predator. Perhaps a protector.

The creature appeared to shift its position. Now it was standing beside the window. So close that were it to lean back and look, it could see her boot on the ledge. She could hear it breathing distinctly now; she could hear it scratching itself. She thought she could hear the turn of its neck as it shifted its gaze and looked out on the ley.

The girl stood rigid. She breathed in dead whisper. Her eyes wide open and wary. She felt reassured by the thorn beneath her, which spread like a natural defence, like a shield, to stop the creature's advance. Yet, perversely, she wanted to be found out; she wanted the creature to come. She would rather their first meeting wasn't like this – here, exposed on a shelf. But she yearned to know what it was so much – so much that she might have revealed herself. So much, that she nearly stood up. She would have done too, if it weren't for the fact – so clear in her mind, so keen to her sense – that she needed first sight of the beast. That first sight would tell her all that she needed. She would know what to do as soon as she saw it. So as not to frighten the creature away; nor yet to find herself being its prey.

The beast was moving again. It was moving away from the ruin at speed, as if in sudden pursuit. She knew enough to know it was going; she knew it wouldn't look back. She was safe. Cautiously, she shifted her feet, pivoting on the slender shelf till she was facing the slate. Then she raised her head above the wall. She looked out.

For the first time, she had a clear sight of the creature. She saw it in entirety. Its legs, its torso, its head. Skulking away, with its back towards her. Slinking in and out of the scrub.

It was a man. A man in grey-green clothes. He was marching away and moving swiftly, his feet appearing to glide through the grass, a bag slung over his shoulder.

For a moment she needed to move her feet. She glanced down to look at the shelf. When she raised her head again, he had vanished. There was no trace of him on the path. He had gone. The girl watched and waited. She held her breath in the breathless wind, waiting for him to come back into sight. But he didn't. Along the path was no movement, no sound. There was nothing above, there was nothing beyond, the shifting and nodding of reeds.

After a while she got down from her shelf and scratched through the bramble onto the path. She traced the man's steps till she stood exactly in the place where she thought she had seen him last. She looked up the bank. Here it was grassy and barren of bushes. There wasn't anywhere he might hide. She tested the ground with the tip of her shoe, thinking there might be a hole. But there wasn't. Then she looked in the last remaining direction. The reeds were massive; they couldn't be breached. They were swirling and singing through frosted lips, teasing and mocking, refusing to tell.

Does anyone live in the ley?
Don't be stupid. No one can live in the ley. Why would anyone want to?
If they were an escaped convict or something?
Honestly! No one can live in the ley. It's a river. A marsh. There's nothing down there. It's cold and windy and wet. You wouldn't survive if you tried to live there. You would be mad if you tried.

Does anyone go down there?

Why should anyone go down there?

I don't know. They might.

What for? There's nothing to do in the ley.

Have you ever seen anyone there?

Never. Why? Have you?

No.

Then why do you ask?

I was wondering if you could get through the reeds.

Ha! You were wondering if you could walk on water!

Perhaps. Have you ever been down there?

I can't say I've been all the way to the reeds. Before they put up the fence, I probably got quite close. But it's a cold and empty place. There's no reason to go anywhere near when you can take the path through the field.

Why did they put up the fence?

For safety's sake. It's boggy down there. And in the winter, it floods. If you fell in the water you'd drown.

Then why's it here? Why don't they drain it?

It's here because it is here. It's always been here. Long before houses and people came. Why should they drain it? That's costly. Besides, nature would come and reclaim it once more, flooding it over again. It's wild. It's neither the land nor the sea. That's why they call it the ley.

The next morning the girl walked down the field to the fence, following her route to the sea. She guessed that the man had seen her before; he had seen her going to swim. He probably knew her in much the same way as she had come to know him. As a creature of curious routine. When she came to the fence, she stopped and listened. She looked both ways up the track. The time was right for him to be here. She knew him somewhere close by.

She ambled forward – a few more paces – feeling self-conscious for being marooned, here in the field and stood in a bathrobe, holding her towel in her hand. She continued; she waited; she went on once more. She knelt down, tying imaginary laces, finding excuses to stop.

Looking along the line of the fence, she saw with dismay the dunes were nearby. Then, briefly, at the fringe of her sight, she thought she could see a shiver of reeds, a clatter as they opened and closed.

She swivelled round to confront the ley. It lisped its secrets smilingly, knowing its words meant nothing to her, knowing its secrets untold. She walked on. And now she had reached the head of the path which led up the dune to the beach, with the ley receding behind her.

Half an hour later, she returned from her swim. The girl was dawdling along the fence despite the feeling of cold. She needed to know where he was. Each time she came to one of the posts, she kicked it out of frustration. It felt good releasing her irritation. It felt good for lengthening her journey back home.

Kick. Kick. Kick. Kick.

Then, suddenly, the man was here – as if born from a crack in the earth. He was coming up fast; he was heading towards her. His head, his neck, his shoulders and arms, clear above the roll of the bank. She called –

Hello!

He was moving briskly. He was downwind of her. She raised her voice and shouted –

Good morning!

She waved. She thought she saw him glance up and see her. On meeting his eye, she smiled. And, just as she smiled, he was hidden by bush. Then where, seconds later, he should have emerged – he was gone.

He was gone.

Perhaps there was a dip in the bank. Perhaps he had stumbled. But she knew that neither of these could be true. He had disappeared. He had vanished again. Only this time, she knew his avoidance was conscious. He had deliberately stolen away.

There was no doubt in her mind that he must have seen her. It was certain he would have heard her calling. Then why did he fail to respond? Why didn't he wave? She hurried up to the fence; she looked down the bank to where he had been. He was definitely no longer there. He had wilfully chosen not to engage. He was intent on being alone. She was separate; she was not of his world. He was excluding her from it. The fence might as well have been an ocean, an infinite void of space, of time. He lived an existence removed from her own, and she was trapped where she was. Two parallel worlds that never could meet. She knew that in order to know what he was, she would need to abandon her world entirely. Only then could she enter his.

The girl was not afraid to cross over. She knew the ley; she felt it was hers. Yet all she knew was the man-made structure: the ruin which lay between both worlds. While what he knew was the essence of nature – the bank, the bushes, the reeds – and he seemed to know it so well. In crossing, she realised that all she knew, that all she was and who she was, would fundamentally have to change.

It would have to change, though she wasn't sure how. Whilst she remained in the timid field, whilst she walked down to the beach in her bathrobe, she was just a ten-year-old girl. A girl who liked swimming, who ran with the wind. But transposed to the ley, she would need to become him, to mirror his movement and catch him by stealth. By ignoring her, he had made her the hunter. He had made himself into the prey.

She knew he was active at dusk and at dawn. By day the ley was all hers. At noon that day she went to the beach and gathered a handful of stones. Then she climbed the dune and entered the ley, tracing the path she had seen him take on the unseen track by its fringe. She proceeded with care. From time to time she left the trail, she paused to inspect a patch of scrub – a low-hanging bush with a darkened core, a natural hollow buried by grass – and marked it out with a stone. When she came to the ruin, she stopped. There were three stones left in her hand. Slowly the girl retraced her steps, spotting her markers laid in the grass – now, when seen from this other direction – noting the hideout they marked.

Then, for a second time, she set out from the dune. Now she practised the hunt. She practised creeping from hide to hide, running low, without sound. She practised wriggling into each lair without disturbing the leaves. She practised slipping out of their comfort. Swiftly, invisibly, soundless. She practised seeing without being seen. When she was done, she dug more trenches under the fence, then she covered them over with grass.

After tea she returned to the field. She was wearing a grey woollen cap, and a dark green cotton jacket and trousers.

Her pockets were both filled with pebbles. She walked towards the sea by the fence, watching out for the man. At the base of the dune, she slipped round the wire and ran down the track till she reached her first marker. She crept into a bush to its side.

For half an hour, she lay in wait. Then she heard the sweep of his feet. His footfall was familiar now: his tread revealing his distance, his speed. She rose without motion into a crouch, waiting for him to arrive. Then he was here – he was right beside her – only four feet away from her side. He was moving swiftly while watching the reeds. She paused to wait till he passed. Five, ten, fifteen paces. When she counted to twenty, she broke from her cover, flinging herself down the bank with the softest of sound. She could see him rounding a bend. She set out behind him, bent hunching and low. She slipped to her stomach as she came to a rise, her face smudged into the earth.

She glanced up. He was thirty paces in front of her now. He was looking out at the reeds. Not over the reeds but seemingly at them, as if staring into their heart. Then he was off, moving faster than ever. She waited until he had rounded a bush, then she got to her feet and sprinted behind him, showering a sprinkling of stones from her pocket at the place where she saw him last stop.

She ran straight past her second marker, and then beyond to her third. She dropped to the earth as she came to the bush, straining hard to draw breath. She hoped he wasn't still there – just beyond her – on the farther side of the shrub. She hoped he wouldn't turn back. She felt faint from the chase, and her limbs felt swollen. She took a final gulp of air, then snaked her way round the bush.

She could see him – but only just see him. He was more than a hundred yards in the distance, charging on down the track. She rolled on her back and closed her eyes. She undid her jacket and pulled up her shirt, fanning herself with its flaps. He was too fast for her and she couldn't keep up. She knew this was no way to trap him.

Early next morning she entered the ley; she buried herself in the last of her hides. She waited, counting the stones in her pockets, convincing herself that she had the strength, that she had the speed and the stealth to follow. The day was cold. Mist coiled around the bite in the earth where she lay on the dew-wet bank. The reeds were grey and darkened by shadows; they were almost black at their core. She could hear them curse through their teeth.

As the sun emitted a faltering beam on the virgin track at the foot of the bank, she saw the man was approaching. He was moving swiftly, tireless and even, like a deer might glide over clumps of heather, his body alert to all sound. He came straight towards her, as if he had spied her, though she knew she couldn't be seen. She listened to the crush of his tread. It was confident, measured, assured. Now he was here – before her, beside her – now passing by, unawares. Now fifty yards farther on. And there, of a sudden, he halted. He looked out over the ley.

The girl rose into a crouch, watching the man as he stood quite rigid, quite still, in an infinite pocket of time. He was staring before him – he seemed to be listening – his head slightly cocked to one side. In his right hand he held a pair of binoculars; his left arm hung useless and limp. The bag on his shoulder was strung with small sacks. They were white, and they danced in the wind.

He turned towards her again. He was coming back down the path. She forced herself yet further and deeper into the heart of her hide. She judged where he was by the sound of his tread, by the sound of his breath, by his shadow. He passed her once more, but now he was moving deliberately cautious and slow. Every twenty-five yards he stopped and looked up, searching over the ley.

This was a pace she could match. A rhythm, a melody, of regular movement. He walked, he watched, he moved on. The girl slipped out from under her cover; she kept her distance in following behind him, sneaking from hide to hide in his wake. For a while they continued – together, distinct – united in their separate quests. In the secret universe that they shared. The girl felt the comforting flow of their motion – as steady and even as drawing breath, as the pulse of the blood through her veins.

Then, as they entered a seventh cycle, she stopped to look up from her hide. The man had vanished again.

The girl scanned and scoured the grassy contours – each furrow, each burrow, each nook. He was not ahead; he had not doubled back; he had not climbed onto the bank. He had to be in the reeds. She stared at the ley without comprehension. She could not believe he had gone there. Yet she crouched, expectant, for knowing he must have. She waited for him to come out. She waited. She waited so long that the sun rose in full, till it danced on the mirror of the sea. Its brilliance distracted her for an instant, and she turned to follow its sheen.

There, silhouetted against the sky, on the dune on the farther side of the ley, was a distant shape that she knew to be him. A blurred black dot, moving steadily away.

It was afternoon. The girl was hidden deep in the heart of the hide that lay by the ruin. He would not escape her again. She told herself he would not. She twisted the grass between her fingers, as she watched out for him on the track. When she spied him coming up from the dunes, she could see he was moving at speed. As soon as he passed her, she got to her feet. She knew he wouldn't stop till he turned. She knew he wouldn't look back.

The girl rolled out of her hide, lying low at the base of the bank, watching him from behind. On the farther side of the ruin, he stopped. He turned to study the reeds. She looked at him with the same sharp interest. Each movement he made was exact and precise; identical to the previous day; pared down to the simplest of actions. All that he did was laden with purpose; none of his actions made sense. She watched him keenly. His every movement. Breathing as he did. Becoming one. Now he was working back to the dune, stopping at intervals, just as that morning. She snaked back into her hide. Now I will see you. This time I will see you. Now I will unearth your secrets. She watched him and watched him – lidless, unblinking – never taking her eyes from the man.

He came past her again in his own fluid rhythm, close by the fringe of the ley. Ten paces beyond, he turned down the bank, he parted the reeds, he was gone. For an instant, the close stems sung out a shocked music, then their cacophony hushed, they rejoined the chill choir.

The girl ran forward and reached to her pocket to mark the spot with a scatter of stones. She felt safe, for she knew he wouldn't come back. From the track she stared at the thatch of reeds, seeking inside it, seeking within.

She could see nothing. She came closer towards them, lifting her hand. But on lifting her hand they came alive, shrieking at her, and butting their heads, and shivering the blades of their leaves. She fell back onto the bank.

She looked up. It was twilight. Darkness had enveloped the land. Stray clouds drifted high like smoke, wafted from the blaze of the day. She dared not trespass into their midst. She would have to wait till the dawn.

That night she couldn't sleep. She pictured herself as she crept in his footsteps, following him blindly into the reeds. Again and again and again. How was she able to walk on the water? How could the reeds give way before her? How could she trust this stranger, this creature? How could she welcome this exquisite danger? She lay back, closing her eyes. She could see herself now, being choked by the reeds, being starved of air as they crowded around her. She could see their fierce stems stretching towards her, weaving their sinews around her neck. Their sharpened edges slicing her legs till the ley was red with her blood. She could see herself drowned, looking back through the water, beyond their tips, to a crack of blue sky. And she cried and cried till the ley was filled – till the reeds were up to their necks in her tears – till channels of briny water arose and flooded the world where she sank.

Morning. The girl sat in a bite in the earth, close by the clasp of stones she had sprinkled to mark where he entered the reeds. He was coming. She could hear him approach from the dune. She watched the man as he strode straight past her, onwards until he came to the ruin. She watched as he made his gradual return. It was all familiar to her now. It was all so known, yet unclear.

At the very point where her stones were laid, he cut to the left with the same steady pace, he melted away in the reeds.

The girl came out from her hide. The nascent day lay empty before her, ready for her to do as she must. To follow the man, to find him out. Yet the day seemed scarcely sufficient. She knelt beside her scatter of stones and looked straight into the reeds. In the skulking light of the creeping dawn, they were awesome, unfriendly, cold. They didn't want her; they wouldn't yield. To him, maybe, but not her. Perhaps she should wait until the sun had burnt its mark on their brittle backs, till they sweated and sighed and lost their hatred. Then perhaps she could try. As she sat by the reeds she could hear them speaking. They were constantly chattering; nudging each other; mocking her with forked tongues. She won't do it. She doesn't dare. She's afraid of us. She thinks she'll drown in our brackish water. She thinks she'll drown. She'll drown.

I'm not afraid of you! I'm not! If the man can find a path through the ley, then so can I. And I will!

She stood abruptly, trembling with fury. She thrust her blinded arms in the reeds just at the point where her stones were laid. She pulled the cruel stems apart. In front of her was a stretch of water, and beyond it several more. A path was woven between each stream – bridges of reed bent over itself, buoyed on the water, bone-white. A teasing slush of water ran between her and the first of the flimsy bridges, two feet wide at the narrowest point. She heard it speaking to her. If you step over us and onto the reeds you will die. It will sink with your weight, and so will you. You will enter our world. You will drown.

She looked at the reed bridge, cackling and jeering. She looked at the bottomless oily brown water. For an instant, she glanced at the field, at the sky. She took one last look at the world that she knew. Then she jumped.

She landed squarely on the bent spine. It shuddered and yawned, yet it held her. She could feel it yield beneath her feet, as if she were somehow floating upon it. It wasn't firm, yet she didn't sink. Instinctively, before she could think, she leapt again to the second bridge. And then to the next, and the next. Each time she hurdled a channel of water. And now she was ten straits deep in the ley. So far within she could see above the crested tassels back to the field. She could even see the distant farm. All around her the reeds were bristling, crowding about her arms and legs. The noise they made was immense. The girl stood still and closed her eyes. She shallowed her breath. She counted slowly to thirty. The reeds would not hurt her; they would protect her. She would be safe on the bridges.

Now she knew that she wouldn't drown, but she still didn't know why the man should come here, or why he chose this route through the ley. Why should he take it – from nowhere to nowhere – when he could cross by the dunes on the beach? Or, if not to cross, then why come at all? What was inside that would make him come?

She took more giant strides through the ley, working her way to its heart. She came to a broad expanse of water, flowing swiftly between the bridges. Over the stream was a plank of wood, and on the other side was more path. She knew she had come to the core. This was the very crux of the ley, from which it took form and came into being. This was its soul; it was where life began.

The girl turned, feeling consciously guilty, fearing the ley might fathom her notions, fearing that she might be seen. She studied the reeds that busied around her. In looking back down the path she had come, she could see a spread of narrower paths branching off from the spine. So faint she hadn't seen them before. Down one of the paths, the girl could see two slender posts which rose from the water, reaching over the crested tips. And between the posts was a stretch of netting. So fine it seemed to be woven within the broader fabric of sky.

The girl retraced her steps and entered the offshoot. She brushed past the reeds till she stood by the poles, stretching her hands in the air. The netting was delicate, almost invisible. It fainted and sighed in the breeze. It was elegant; utterly beautiful. Irresistibly, she was drawn towards it – her hands around it, and now within. She thought it might tear like a spider's web. But it didn't. It was strong. It held her fingers; it gently ensnared them; it wound its thread round her palms. The girl wriggled out and drew herself free. Released, the netting blew like a sail, fractionally darkening the sparkling sky.

The girl shivered involuntarily. Again, she felt the shock of her fear, the fear of being entangled and caught. She reached to her pocket and scattered some stones to mark where the net had been hidden. Then she retreated across the bridges with a steady and unrelenting motion, till she was safe on the land. As soon as she was clear on the bank, she turned and looked back to where she had come from. There was nothing there. Nothing to show of the path she had been on. Nothing to show of the bridges and water. Nothing to show of the net. Nothing to see but the roll of the reed as it hissed at the anodyne sky.

Evening. The girl crouched close by the pillared netting, deep in the heart of the ley. She was hidden behind a wall of reed, trapped in the constant shadow of dusk that lined the base of the ley. She sat on bone-white, broken reed, bent and stretched across the streams. She was watching the thickening, reddening sky, and the shapeless netting which cut across it. She was listening to the clear, thin breeze which wound through the reeds and was caught in the net.

He was coming. She could hear him. She could hear the reeds were muttering in warning, whispering, passing the news to each other to say he was coming, he was on his way. He was stepping as swiftly over the bridges as he did when he was on land. His tread was confident and sure. Almost as soon as she first heard the sound, she could see him coming towards her. He came to within three feet of her hide, low in the thicket of reeds. So close, she could reach out and touch his boot, she could feel the warmth of his breath.

He turned and began inspecting the net. She could see him plucking the thread with his hands. His right hand busily working the mesh, while his left hand lifted a sack to the net – just for a moment – before bringing it down and drawing it closed, then tying the sack to his bag. He repeated the process three times.

The girl's eyes switched from watching the man to the small white sacks which hung at his waist. She stared at them, searching for meaning. She stared till those sacks were all she could see, till she blocked out the rest of the restless world. And then, as she looked – as she stared at a sack – she saw something moving within it. It hopped.

She was so surprised on seeing it move, she forgot where she was, and who she was with. She gasped.

The man turned around. He came towards her; he started to speak. She couldn't make out what the man was saying, though she could hear his voice was falsetto and thin. She couldn't make sense of the words he spoke, for as soon as he turned she had leapt to her feet. She had leapt to her feet and started to run. She was running now. She was running furiously, jumping the bridges, escaping the man and his huge black shadow which seemed to block out the sky. As she ran, the reeds thrashed out at her body. They were slashing her face; they were strangling her arms; they were tugging her back by her legs. They were laughing because they knew that the man would be much faster than her. They knew that in time he was sure to catch her. It was only a matter of when.

Then, of a sudden, she found herself falling, unable to stifle her fall. She was on her side, with her face in the water. She tried to raise herself with her arms; she tried to kick her legs free. But all her limbs were shackled about her. The more she thrashed, the tighter her bonds. She strove to raise her head from the stream. She was close to a bridge, but not on it. She could feel herself sinking into the ley. She was sobbing, dissolving: her pitiful tears diluting the glutinous brine. She could taste its salt in her mouth.

Then he was there. He was lifting her free; he was lifting her body clear of the water. He was untangling her legs from the capture of nets. He was carrying her through and out of the reeds, along the path and up to the bank.

He was lying her down in the sedge. He was parting the hair which clung to her face and looking into her eyes.

The twilight sky was huge and red. The reeds were a solid mass: a curling threatening scream of hate. She saw him bending over her; she saw him coming near. In panic, she summoned all her strength. All the strength in her sinews. She crab-crawled up the clumps of grass; she stood; she scrambled up the bank. She scratched at the turf beneath the fence; she slid back through her shallow grave; she headed up the slope of the field, over the gate and into the farm, without once looking behind.

The Trapping

The next morning, the girl helped her aunt with the rounds. She hung close to her; she was thin like a shadow; she was timid and had little to say. In the shy clear morning air, she looked ghostlike and pale. The aunt felt like dropping her tools in the yard and running to smother her deep in a hug. To breathe vital warmth back into her hands. To kiss her, to fire her to life.

After breakfast, the girl didn't go for a swim. Nor did she skip away down the field like a giddy gust of fresh air. Instead, she stayed close, she stayed tight to the farm. She stayed near the animals, near to her aunt. Perhaps she was feeling unwell.

The girl didn't know what she felt. She couldn't explain the thing she was feeling, nor did she know why she felt it. All she could know was the feeling itself; a feeling that washed its bile through her veins; a feeling consuming her soul. A feeling at times almost abstract, remote; at times so close she could reach out and touch it. An incisive and absolute fear. So irrational and so intense, she didn't know how to vent nor tame it. A fear defying all description; indistinct save for a single truth. The man. The man. And what that man did, or what he might do. The knowing and not knowing what that might be. The shock of the water in her face, the immensity of the solid night, the wave after wave of screaming reed. The memory, the touch of his hands. The sensation she felt – of feeling him brush her hair from her face, of seeing him standing over her. His presence blocking the vestige of twilight, imprisoning her in interminable shade.

And alongside the fear, she felt a revulsion. Something so outright she swore to herself she would never go to the ruin again. She would never re-enter the ley. She told herself she would keep to the worlds which belonged to her and her aunt. She would hold herself back and vanish away; she would no longer go where the man might be lurking, or where she might see him again. It was not that she feared the man in himself. What she feared was all that she couldn't see; what she didn't know of the man. Who he was, what he did, and what he might do. The only thing that she definitely knew was the feeling of being as he loomed above her, as he leant towards her, as he lifted her up. The feeling of feeling his hands. That single image shattered her reason, creating foreboding of infinite weight beside the enigma of who he was, or the secrets that stirred in the ley. Her sinewy body shuddered its loathing, knowing that it had been caught. She, the hunter, who had entered his world. She had been hunted, ensnared.

And still, in the deep recess of her mind, in the shivering heart of her haunted being – despite all the oaths that she made to herself – she sensed that now she was trapped.

For a second day the girl clung to her aunt, eager to be on the farm. She hugged the same space, like one of the dogs, wanting only the warmth of attention, wanting the comfort of closeness. Her aunt could tell there was something amiss, something within her that needed her. She opened wide that welcoming space; she gave her heart and her time. She filled the void that was empty of words with a shameless and unvoiced love. They baked scones together; they dug up potatoes; they took the dogs scenting for rabbits.

In the afternoon the girl climbed her tree. She clambered high up through the golden-green leaves so she could sit without being seen. She thrust her arms between the boughs to open new portholes into the world and spy down onto the yard. She saw Henry's head standing proud of his stable; she saw a dog on the porch that was scratching; she saw a cat steal out of the barn, a wounded mouse in its jaws. It was all so familiar to her now, so reassuring and sure. But it felt detached and removed. As though she was looking on from afar – looking onto and into the world that she knew – without being within it herself. As though she was no longer part of its structure. As though she was separate and not safe within it. She was alone: alone in her tree. She was alone and in hiding. Unconnected from all of that being; from everything else that there was.

Unthinkingly, she swivelled around, opening a new window into the leaves so she could look out at the sea. There it lay, serene in the distance; so far away it was silent and smooth, like a mirror reflecting the sky. From the sea her gaze was drawn to the ley. It too was silent; it scarcely moved. She could see the chimney and the walls of the ruin. Like the farm, they also seemed distant. They seemed distant, yet – unlike the farmyard – they weren't divorced from herself. Instead, she felt they were there at her core – that her soul still sat on the ruin's walls, that it lay at the foot of the reeds. It was there that she was. It was there not here. Torn from the ley, she was incomplete, she was something less than herself. She stared and stared at the ley. She knew she was here, sitting here in this tree. Yet all of her being felt she was there – really there – surrounded by chattering reeds.

Again, on the following day, she climbed the Judas tree after breakfast. She inspected the yard with a fleeting glance, and then she turned to the ley. She looked at it steadily, her eyes unswerving. She looked until she could see it breathing – its long, prone body drawing in air. Until she could trace the rise and fall of its tortured ribcage, its lungs. Until she could hear its faint exhale as it puffed at the sparkling sea. She sensed the distance being swallowed to nothing. She could hear its shivering core; she could lay her hand on its heaving chest and feel the beat of its heart. Come to me. Be with me. You are a part of me. She looked at it blindly, with certainty, longing. She looked, and in looking she saw she was there. She was there, she was looking back on herself – at a lost lonely girl hiding up in a tree.

The girl looked out and onto the ley. She wasn't looking for something within it, just looking at it as it was. Living it, feeling it, being a part. The field collapsed, it was falling away. And now it was her, just her and the ley, bridging the distance, fusing together, becoming inseparable, melding as one.

It was then she saw something else. Unwittingly, in that intimate moment, something specific distracted her gaze. It was him. The man. She could see him. And something was wrong. To begin with she couldn't work out what it was, for she saw he was walking beside the ley, much as she always had seen him. But something seemed out of place. Though she ached not to look, she needed to see.

It was then that she realised what was wrong. He wasn't in the ley at all. He was walking beside the fence in the field. She saw him come through the gap in the hedge.

She saw him walking across the next field. Now he was cutting his way up the slope. He was coming straight for the farm. He was coming for her. Here, right now – in the fierce light of day – away from the comfort, the stealth of the ley. She knew he was coming for her.

The girl was high in the tree; she was hidden from sight. No one could know where she was. No one could reach her, and no one could seize her. No one, she told herself. No one.

The girl looked down at the ground. She looked through the dim web of branches that trapped her; she sensed that within them there could be no escape. No. He would know where she was. He would find her out. She knew that he would. She knew it was true. In that moment, the animals, the courtyard, her aunt, and the farm – all of it, all that she knew and she loved – sank out of sight beneath her. She was there on her own, in the broken bones, in the skeleton of a winter tree, utterly at his mercy. She was there alone, she was all on her own, and she didn't know what she could do. She sensed there was nothing to use as a shield. And caught in that nothing, she sat unbreathing, awaiting the thing that must come.

Halfway up the field, the man stopped. He was now so close that the girl could see his eyes were fixed on the slope. He was looking directly towards the farm. Not just at the farm, but at her tree. She could feel his gaze scorch holes through the leaves, denuding the tree and leaving her bare – stupid, marooned on the twisted boughs.

For an instant, the man looked down at his hand. She could see there was something clasped in his grip. He looked from his fist back up to the farm. Then he halted.

He stood transfixed in the field. In the sun. In that single breath, both chilling and helpless. Somehow, both those sensations together. Coiled round each other, biting their necks, waiting to see which would die. He had come to get her, as he had before. He knew where she was, and no one could stop him. He would not rest until he was here, standing above her, reaching towards her. Till all she could see was the shape of his head, his face without feature or form. She knew he would come. He had to come. Yet right now he seemed vulnerable, anxious. Exposed in the field – in a foreign world – as trapped as her: just as awkward. She knew he preferred to hide in the ley, to burrow within its furious shelter, knowing that there he was safe. And in that instant of knowing the truth, she almost felt sorry for him.

The man looked up one more time. One final time. Then he turned and trudged away down the field, back towards the fence and the dune.

That night, the girl lay in bed in her room on the ground floor next to the kitchen. She lay awake and stared through the pitch, reassured by the line of electric light which split the door from the floor. In her mind, she was reliving her day, watching it over, in infinite detail, as if by watching she could make it make sense. She turned to the curtainless window to console herself in the moon. But instead of seeing the moon, she saw the face of the man. His face. It was staring in at her own. Like the moon, it appeared both silver and grey. And, just like the moon, it stood suspended, hung in the frigid sky, unmoving. Not even the eyes seemed to move. Then, it was gone. It was gone in a moment. Leaving nothing behind. No more than the shapelessness of the blackness.

The darkness of vacant, unfathomable night. The girl could feel the pulse of her heart, the air in the shallow cage of her lungs. And now she could hear his tread. His footfall, which had grown so familiar she could use it to judge his pace and direction, as he came round the side of the house to the front. The door would be locked, of course. But the door wasn't locked. She could hear a click as the handle turned. She could hear a creak as it opened and closed. She could hear his tread on the flags outside. She could see a break in the line of light – that light which split the door from the floor. Broken by the legs of the man as he stood on the farther side.

The girl awoke. She turned instinctively to the window and saw that the curtains were closed. She rose from her bed and opened her door, walking down the corridor to test the lock and the key. The door was fast. She returned to her room; she climbed into bed; she rolled her body into a ball. And there, in the darkness, the loneliness, she hugged herself to herself.

The next morning, the girl hung close to her aunt, she clung to the simple routine. She helped milk the cows; she fed Henry a carrot; she made a bucket of slop for the pig; she gave bowls of food to the dogs.

When all the morning's chores were done, they went together back to the kitchen, and there together they ate. The girl seemed unwilling to leave the house, while appearing restless within it. She looked out onto the luminous day from within the shadow of every room. Eventually, she opened the door, driving the dogs out into the yard before daring to come out herself. She ran straight up to Judas tree and hid herself in its boughs.

The girl sat in the harbouring branches, knowing herself blind and unseen. She opened no windows between the knit boughs, but sat in the deep of their dismal world which shifted from shadow to shafting light. The leaves around her played like children, fickle and frantic and carefree. They danced delighted, as the reedbed could not. Theirs was a splendid innocence, an ignorance, an undilutable bliss. Stung with no secrets, no shame. Theirs was a simple song of pure joy, sung over and over again.

Above the giddy laughter of leaves, the girl could hear the sound of two voices. She pushed her feet against a bough to open a sliver of world. She could see her aunt. She had come to the porch. And now she was walking into the yard. The girl shifted position to keep her in sight. Her aunt took a few paces forward, then stopped. The girl pressed more weight on the arm of the bough so the window before her grew wide. She kicked out her legs to splay the branches, parting the whispering leaves.

And now, she could see the whole yard. There was her aunt, her hand to her forehead, shielding the sun from her eyes. And there before her – in the plain light of day – there in front of her, was the man. He was there, in the courtyard. The man –

Hello. Is there a girl living here? I thought I had seen a girl.
Yes, my niece lives here. How can I help you?
I'm sorry to intrude. I thought she might like animals.
Yes, she does.
I thought she might like this.
What is it? Where? O, it's beautiful! Where did you get it?

From the ley.

Really? How lovely. Yes, I'm sure she would love to see it. It's gorgeous. I've never seen one of these up close. She's somewhere round here, on the farm.

The girl sat rigid in her tree. She could see them standing in the yard through the strip of window she had made in the leaves. She could see them as they continued talking, but her head seemed to spin, and, in her confusion, she lost the sense their words. She lost sight of where she was, too. She lost all sense of who she was, and of what was happening around her. Something within her, something beyond her, had paralysed her and arrested her being. It was numbing her mind and her senses.

It was the man. He was here in the yard. He had come for her. He had come. Yet it seemed he had come to show her something, not to do something to her. He had something with him he had shown her aunt — something she thought was beautiful — something her aunt said that she would like too. If only the girl could see it from here, without the need to climb down. But she couldn't. She couldn't see it; she couldn't get down. Yet she had to. She had to do both. He had something with him that had come from the ley. Something she needed to see. The smallest fraction of life from the ley had come to the yard to see her. Even now, it was out there, calling to her. It didn't matter what it might be. It didn't matter who brought it. It had come for her, and she needed to see it. She needed to break from her hide. To go outside. Her aunt would stay out there in the yard — there to protect her and keep her safe. Her aunt wouldn't leave her alone with this man. She wouldn't be left on her own.

The girl's desire was overwhelming. She felt herself slip off her bough. Now she was climbing down the tree; her feet were stretching, were touching the ground; her feet were carrying her over the courtyard, over to where her aunt was waiting. And now she was standing awkwardly, shielding herself in the smudged caress, in the sheltering folds of her aunt's frayed dress.

The man was standing in front of her, only the stretch of an arm away. No more than the stretch of his arm. In the fullness of day, away from the ley, he looked ordinary. Less than that. Weak. He was thin, and about the same height as her aunt. His manner was twitchy and nervous. His eyes, his hands – in fact, all of his movements – were restless but quick, like a bird's. She could feel that he was looking straight at her; she could feel his eyes on her face. She felt a loss of control of her limbs, a dullness dumbing her mind. As if she was dreaming, not fully awake. Then she felt her aunt lay her hands on her shoulders, bringing her out from the shield of her apron, standing her out on her own, near the man.

The girl looked down at the ground. She stared at it hard. From the corner of her eye, she could see his cupped hands stretching out and coming towards her. Gradually, irresistibly closer. As hard as she looked at the concrete courtyard, she had to see what it was.

The man dropped one of his hands to his side, and there, in the other, peeping out through his fingers, was a small blue feathery head. Startling, brilliant, electric blue. With fierce black eyes, a long stout beak. She knew what the bird was at once. It was a kingfisher. For a moment, it seemed stunned by the shock of the light, as the man removed his hand from its eyes. Then it seemed to agitate into life, looking about it restlessly with swift, jerking moves of its head. Its beak was strong, yet the way that he held it was such that it couldn't reach out and nip him, nor could it escape from his hand. It was couched and cradled so comfortably it looked quite content where it was. As if the bird had found a new perch – one that was harmless and warm. The man slowly twisted his wrist and the bird, and now the girl and her aunt could see the delicate body in full. They could see the amber flush of its belly, the fierce white streak of its neck. The girl felt an urge to reach out and touch it. She wanted to feel its shimmering blue head, its fragile body urgent with life.

Before she could move, she felt the man's hand reach out and latch on her own. It was a curious clasp. His fingers didn't quite lock around hers. His grip was tight, but he found it hard to move and position his arm. He took her hand and guided her fingers till they rested against the infant crest of the bird's astonished head. The feathers were painfully soft. She felt as if the skull might break simply with the weight of her touch. Then he folded her hand within his own so that now she too was holding the bird; she too could feel the warmth of its belly; she too could feel the tiny heart beating out on her palm. The man turned his hand to face back upwards. He opened his fingers, seeming to know that her hand would mirror his own. For an infinite fraction, a fragment of time, the bird sat, stumpy, ecstatically blue, on their hands. Then it flapped its short wings, and it flew – dipping and weaving and diving low flight – out through the courtyard, over the gate, and down the slope to the ley.

The girl gasped. She pulled away from the man and ran after, urging her body to fly like the bird's, to dart to the ley, to be free. She stood at the gate and panted her joy, watching the bird till she saw it no more. Till she could only imagine its body brushing the delicate tips of the reeds, searching within for its nest. Then deeper still. She could feel herself in the ley with the bird, living the harmony of the reeds, riding them as they shrieked in the wind, seeking out insects with luminous eyes. She felt herself diving through pools of brown water, skewering a fish with her beak. She pushed back her head, she opened her throat, and gulped it greedily in. She felt the ecstasy of low flight, of bobbing and cutting a path through the reeds. She felt the morning mists rising as steam, being burnt off by the sun. She felt the trembling chill of the night pressing its ice on the lips of the ley. She felt summer and winter, death and renewal. A lifetime of freedom, a lifetime of being, a lifetime of cold solitude.

When, at last, she turned to the yard, she saw her aunt was standing alone. They came together knowingly, smiling a secretive joy. Her aunt had found out much from the man. He had caught the kingfisher in a net that he had placed in the reeds. That's what he told her he did. He trapped birds to study them before he released them. He had found a way of entering the ley; of moving within, through the reeds. For years he had been here, watching the birds, though it seemed he had never been seen. He had come to the farm to show her the bird, because he thought the girl wanted to see. He had come to ask if she wanted to join him, to go with him in the early mornings. To help him, to watch, to study, to hold, to release the birds that were trapped in his nets.

The girl was listening no more. She was looking over her aunt's aproned shoulder. She was looking beyond her, over the gate and down the slope of the field. She was looking along the foot of the valley. She was staring down at the ley. She was breathing it in – that other world, that world where people did not go, that world ruled by nature alone. Where she could shed the skin of humanity; where she could shed the weight of mortality; where she could lose herself in entirety. Completely, forever, for good.

The dogs were still asleep by the Aga, the farm still clothed in silence and shadow, the whole world indistinct and grey, when she rose the following day. She had awoken long before dawn. She had lain in bed and held her breath, listening to the hollow wind scraping its fingers against the farm, thinking how brittle reeds would be faring, sleepless and restless and yearning for light.

Daybreak was bitter and cold. The wind was slight, but chilled to the soul. She wore a sweater under her jacket, and a grey woollen cap pulled over her brow. As she came to the field she blew on her hands, watching the steam of her breath on the air. The sky was still more darkness than dawn. The field was an unfathomable pool she trod with stumbling, feeling feet. The wetness crackling under her tread. She heard the reeds before she could see them; she heard their murmur, their lisping tips through the thin film of mist which masked the slope. The girl thrust her hands deep into her pockets, turning her face from the gasping breeze, relying on instinct to steer her safe through the gaps in the earth-hedge that led to the sea.

The girl stood alone on the top of the dune, awaiting the approach of the man. It was inconceivable that someone could be here, that any form of life could awaken and join her here on the sand. Even the sea appeared to be slumbering, washed in a fainting hushed liquid dream, murmuring in its easy sleep, rocking itself into rest. The girl could see, she could hear, no birds. No movement, no shadows, no sounds. She could make out nothing alive. She sensed that nothing could trigger to life before daylight had warmed it and breathed in its lungs.

A faint noise distracted her thoughts. It came from the scrub by the foot of the dune. Following the path of the sound with her eyes, she saw that the man was already here. He was here and waiting for her. Here, in the half-light, in the wind-bitten silence, he looked even less like a man. He was silver-grey, spectral, unreal. Just as the air, and the sea, and the land. His movement mirrored the shape of his speech – fluty, staccato, and slight. He beckoned to her, and once she had joined him he was moving swiftly across the dune, onto the track and down the bank, to the invisible fringe of the ley.

Almost at once the man left the track; he slipped through the bushes and vanished from sight. The girl followed close in his steps, finding herself in a patch of grass with scrub and sedge on all sides. Behind one bush, and seemingly in it – as if the timbers were grown from its boughs – was a low wooden hut with a door to one side, fronted by a long narrow window. She looked around for the man; she guessed him inside. Now she could hear the creak of its floorboards; she could hear him feel through the darkness within. Then he emerged with a bag on his shoulder, and once again they were off.

The girl was aware of the man's routine, she knew his path and the lie of the land, yet she struggled to keep to his pace. It was both the speed at which they were travelling, and the relentlessness of their route. Both conspired to torture her, to humiliate her, to mock her effort. And the man made no concession for her. She stumbled in holes and over roots, lost in the shadows of early dawn. His walk was her run, his ease of movement her tangle of laces and twisted feet. He turned to her only when signalling to her – to be quiet, to keep up, to stop, to crouch low. She sensed him displeased at her harshness of breath, at her rustle of movement, at the weight of her tread. By contrast, he seemed to move without sound, to glide across the contoured land as effortlessly as the wind. Only once they reached the walls of the ruin did they stop and pause to catch breath.

The man stood still, listening, alert. From time to time his head would move – an angular and jerking movement, just as the kingfisher had before – as if he were plucking a sound from the air, like an insect plucked from the sky. He stared at specific parts of the ley, training his binoculars on random patches of reed. His limp left arm was hung to his side, like a clipped wing torn by a hawk. The rest of his body was fierce with motion, even when he was still. Suddenly, he set off again – as though he had overlooked she was there – heading straight for the reeds. He leant into them, and they parted before him. She saw him being sucked into their core. For a moment she stared at the shivering stems, at this place she had never noticed before. For a moment only, for knowing that more and she would be lost, with no hope of return. Without thinking, without looking, she followed him in.

Inside was a path that was built like the others, with living bridges of matted reed bent over a patchwork of streams. The man had sensed she was following him and had slackening his pace so that she could catch up. She found safe passage over the swamp by placing her feet in his vacant steps. Several paces into the ley he halted; he turned abruptly and reached at the sky, inspecting an invisible net with his hand. He stood with his back to her, here in a passage too narrow to stand side by side. What he was doing was hidden from her. She saw only fragments and snatches. A spread of his fingers pecking the mesh; a strain of his left hand snatching a sack and lifting it up towards the net; the same hand tying the sack to his waist. A sack now pulsing with new-born life.

He brushed past the girl and was moving again. Again, she leapt over slivers of bridge, following close in his wake. When back on the track he seemed to move faster. She found herself bound to his brutal pace, beating along the border of reed – so fast that her eyes were blinded by tears, her chest grew heavy and dampened with sweat, her scorched lungs gasping for air. She lost all sense of where they were going; of even, now, where they were. The world spun a giddy dance around her, and all she could do was to watch his feet, matching his steps by stepping inside them as they smudged the dizzying earth.

Again, they parted the curtains of reed. Again, they were swallowed inside. More pathways, more bridges, more pools. She could feel the suction of the stream as it pursed its lips round her boots. Just once his hand reached out towards her, guiding her onto a bridge. Then they were out in the brilliant air; then back again, twisting a route through the riot of the restless, furious reed.

The girl sat on the sharp rush floor, not even caring to look at the man as he tirelessly worked at his net. She tried to steady her breath. Her legs felt numb and had crumbled beneath her. She was kneading them back into life. She needed more time to mend. But even now he was off again, driving them further along the track – yet faster in a mesmeric whirl of reed, and water, and sky. The girl felt bewildered: past sickness, past care. She felt the shame of certain collapse. She opened her mouth to call to the man, to beg him to come to a halt. But her throat was parched; it emitted no sound. The only sound was the shivering reeds, spitting scorn in her face.

Then, in an open patch of grass, her legs gave way and she tumbled sideways, holding her stretching arms out rigid to shield herself from the earth. She looked up, expecting to feel his contempt, but saw he was no longer there. They were back where they started, close to the beach, in the grassy hollow hid from the track, fringed by a border of sedge. And the man had entered his hut.

The sky, in homage to the sun, had shed frosted redness and was tinged with gold: inviting the reeds to take on shape, to assume new colour and form. In the sharpening light he had taken his spoils to examine them in his hut. The girl wanted to follow, to see what he found, to see what he would do next. But her body had buckled, and she lay on the grass, broken, beyond getting up. Just once or twice, she could hear a flutter, she could see his hands as they reached for the window, cupped and close as they came to the light. She could see his palms fold back and then sink, almost as if he was going to pray. And there, in his hands, was a startled shape, a wind-bothered bird. Just for an instant. And then, in the next, it was gone.

Just as she felt sufficiently strong to get to her legs and enter the hut, the man came out to the clearing. He stood before her, he but didn't speak. From his look alone, from the way he stood, she knew that his work was done.

Once more they breathlessly trekked to the ruin; once more they retraced their steps down the track. But they didn't stop to inspect the nets, nor did they stop at the hut. Instead, they went straight to the dune. They stood in silence watching the sun as it rose over fields at the end of the valley, as it blushed its joy on the wakening reeds, sighing and swathed in the slim morning mist.

The trapping that morning was over.

He stammered some words that were lost on the wind; and she, too exhausted to speak in reply, nodded a fleeting farewell. Then he was off, away down the beach. She watched him till he departed. Then she dragged her wretched body home and threw herself on her bed.

The girl slept the sleep of fatigue. Within it, she saw the man's urgent feet, the mark of his boots in the misshapen grass, and her own feet laid in his print. Again and again, the image repeated in vital, visceral detail. She saw herself sat in the body of ley as he pecked at the nets with his curious hands. She saw each reed as a separate shape, its feathered tassel, its thin fierce leaves. She saw the small white dancing sacks hung from the rim of the bag at his side. She saw there were six sacks in all. She saw his fingers spinning the net, cradling a bird in his weightless web, looping a curl of the mesh round its wing, easing the freed bird into a sack, pulling the drawstring closed at its mouth. She saw him again, through a crack in the door, stooping over a long low bench, holding a bird in his hand with such care – with such love – measuring it, lifting it up to inspect, then extending his palms and letting it fly out through the window and back to the ley.

When she awoke, the girl went outside and climbed to the top of her Judas tree. From there she looked out on the ley. It was silent and empty. There was no sign of the man. No trace of humanity scored on its soul. No nets, no paths which wound through the reeds, no track beside them, no hut. It was as it must seem to her aunt – for every moment of every day, for all of her life – deserted.

That afternoon, she went to the ruin. She sat on the wall and played her oboe at the raucous body of reeds. As ever, they bristled their indignation, their angst, their incomprehension. They filled the air with their petty fury, with a promise to rise against her and drown her. The girl hooted back her own shrill music, careless, and fearless, and pregnant with joy. She had been within them; there in amongst them. She knew the life that nurtured them, the floating world from which they grew, the paths that led inside. She knew them not one shifting mass – all faceless, graceless, filled with pain – but as they were, a world entire, flawless as it was. The ley was not a place of death. Or, if of death, then also life. Both life and death in perfect poise. For ever and ever. And without end.

The girl awoke in the night. She awoke to the sound of driving rain, spluttering at her flustered window in a foul and gusting wind. She thought of the reeds as they bent to its fury, howling lament and cowering beneath a brutal, bullying sky. She thought of the birds in the ley: of how they would survive the storm, of how they rode the torment out, tossed in a tottering nest like a ship at sea.

And now, in that thinking, she had slipped from her bed; already she had started to dress. In the hall she put on her waterproofs, then she opened the door and was there in the yard. It was pitch black outside, save for a single light that burned on the wall at the end of the stables. Within that tiny universe, the girl could see sharp slivers of rain cutting, diagonally, into the earth. As she rounded the gate and came to the field, the full force of a pummelling wind thumped into her body, beating her back. Pinpricks of rain were stinging her chin, smacking crude music against her jacket. She lowered her head and hunched her shoulders, steering her steps at the blast. The flares of her storm-shocked waterproof trousers flapped and throbbed like the sound of a motor, driving her on down the field.

In the ley she could see whole patches of reed collapsing beneath the furious gusts – at times so submissive they were prone in the water, then rising again in the teeth of the wind, bearing its hate on their backs. Their wretched scream was an endless crescendo, an interminable shriek which bounced off the skies, which cried up the valley and hid in the earth-hedge, filled with immeasurable pain.

When she came to the dune, she crouched in a hollow tucked in the leeward side. She watched as the ley spewed out its soul. She could hear the crush of the labouring sea – each wave which pounded and shook the fabric of the sheltering nook where she lay. She glanced at the unfathomable skies above her, seeing yet denser, darker shapes descending on the deepening darkness, sweeping irresistibly over the land. There were no stars, and no moon. No hope of life, of light, of day. Here was a dungeon of despair, playing its agonies out before her, screaming ecstatic anguish and grief.

In front of it all stood the man. He had come from the beach and over the dune. In the turmoil, he had arrived unseen. Now he was here, he was standing before her, staring at her as she crouched in the sand, spat at and scorned by the storm. They looked at each other without speaking. Then he beckoned to her, and they rode with the wind, over the dune and along the track, till they reached the sheltering hut.

She watched him go through the door. For a moment she stood in the fist of raw nature, uncertain of what might be in the hut, then she followed him into the blackness. Shielded from the cacophony, the room was awkward and still. The girl stood in the gasping silence, the roof and the floor and the wall one body of indistinguishable black. She could hear the man's breath, his shuffling feet; she could hear the search of his hands. Then he struck a match against the darkness, shocking the hut with light.

She saw him, massive, in silhouette, lighting the wick of a lamp. The flame rose furious, incongruous, conjuring shadows against the walls, revealing the bleak spartan room. There was a bench, a desk, a bag, some books, some implements laid on a shelf. But nothing else she could see. She turned around to the man. He was busy removing his waterproof trousers, hanging them over the desk to dry. She watched, before doing the same. Then they both sat down on the ends of the bench –

You shouldn't be here.
Why not?
It's early. There's a storm.
You're here.

He turned away and looked at the floor, as though unable to grasp her logic, or to find the words to reply. Here was a man, so sure in the reeds, so confident when working his nets. Yet now, so hesitant, so lacking conviction. Even with her, a girl of ten. Uncertain. His speech seemed to mirror his awkward left arm; it was unused and broken, unfit. And now here, in the half-light, here, sat before her, his flighty body was shrinking away –

I didn't think you'd come.
Why not?
You didn't like it yesterday.
You didn't want me to like it. But I liked it all the same.
–
Why did you invite me if you didn't want me here?
The storm should blow over soon. Would you like some soup?
No, thank you.

She watched him take a flask from his bag. She watched as he unscrewed the lid and poured soup into the cup. It looked creamy, warm and thick. She could sense his insides break in a smile as its richness spread its gradual succour through to the tips of his limbs. She could feel the heat which rose from his cup. She could smell its goodness wrapping around him – as surely as a hug from her aunt – and she longed for it greedily.

He had turned away and was staring out through the stretch of window cut in the wall. The storm was lessening, the pitch receding to the indistinct pattern of day. Blotchy and ugly, and all washed out. When he had drained the cup of soup he reached for his waterproof clothes. She understood it was time to go. As she dressed she told herself to be strong; she told herself that she wouldn't be shamed by showing herself weak to the man.

On the track the wind blew into their backs, forcing them, urging them on. The girl's feet raced on the ground beneath her. She tried to slow down by leaning against it, pressing her body into the gale. She feared that a gust might knock her sideways, or thrust her into the man. From the wind-whipped tunnel of her hood, she focused her eyes on his moving feet, on his steady footfall pressed in the grass, while following three paces behind.

He sought early refuge within the reeds. In the ley the water was frantic and fast; bridges seemed softer and smaller, less certain; reeds bent low, and thrashed at their bodies, blocking and battering their path. She lost her foothold, once – just once – and her boot was sucked in a pool. Her momentum carried her torso forwards; she slipped and came to her knees. He turned and looked at her sternly. She pulled herself out without his help; she nodded at him to go on. Instead, he stopped and shouted towards her. He shouted above the shrieking reeds. She bent her head in an effort to hear him –

You – watch – step – dangerous.
I know.
The water – dangerous.
I know.
You – be careful. If you fall – water – drown.
I understand.
Can't swim – drown. Stay – path.
Yes.

He continued on, pushing his way through the tortured reeds till they came to a tall sail of netting. It was empty. They returned to the track, blown towards the beaten ruin by the unforgiving wrath of the wind. The girl followed dutifully in his steps, punching a path in his wake. She was angry. Angry more than ashamed. Angry for thinking he thought her weak; angry for knowing he saw her stumble; angry for sensing him angry with her. Why should he be so hard on her? She felt the tears of mute self-pity rise unchecked from deep inside; she felt an annoyance she couldn't suppress. An indignation. She knew the danger. Of course she knew. She knew if she fell she'd be carried away – she'd be borne beneath the mantle of reed – regardless of whether or not she could swim. That was the truth. The beginning and end. Nothing could save her. Not even him.

The man had stopped at the mouth of a reed path, close to the side of the ruin. He turned and looked at the girl. He gave her a look that spoke without words, which told her to stay on the bank. She refused to meet with his eyes. Instead, she waited until he was gone, she waited until he couldn't see, then she tailed swiftly behind him.

They came to a net, and there, distinctly, she saw the shape of a captured bird, just above the tips of the reed. It wasn't struggling – it was lying inert – it was twitching and swaying randomly as the net ballooned in the wind.

This path was broader than most of the others, allowing the girl to come up close to watch the man as he worked. His right hand wove the delicate netting away from the limbs that were snared within it, whilst his left hand stretched towards his bag to pluck out one of the sacks.

Out it came, and just as it came, it escaped from his fingers and fell to the ground. The girl stooped swiftly to catch it up and handed it back to the man. He looked at her briefly; he took it from her. Then he placed the bird he had caught inside, and he tied the sack to his waist. They continued, inspecting two further nets, and finding both had caught birds. Then they turned back into the fragile dawn; they retraced their path to the hut.

The wind was dying, and a hint of light was reflecting off the swollen clouds, as they entered their hidden retreat. The man laid his bag on the bench with care, so the dancing sacks hung free to its side. She counted five sacks in all. They removed their outer waterproof clothing, then she watched as he reached and took down from the shelf a book and a small clutch of tools.

The girl sat down on the bench. Not close to the man, but at an angle from where she could see all he did. She saw him open and flick through his book; she saw him lay out his tools with precision. She saw his actions were quick, but not hurried. She saw his right hand pick up a sack, and his fingers feel blindly within. She saw the sack as it fell away, and there in his clasp was a bird. She saw its head and breast were yellow, its wings and back an infinite blend of yellow and green and brown. She saw its tail was thin and long. Its legs like delicate twigs.

The man looked over the bird minutely. He teased its tucked wing into a stretch, then laid it out against a ruler to measure the length of its span. He put the bird back in its sack, then hung the sack from a metal tube. As the sack pulled down so the tube extended, giving a measure of weight. He took up his pen and turned to his book.

He wrote 'yellow wagtail' there on the page. And in the columns that lay to its side, he recorded the weight, the wingspan, the age. The date and the time that they caught it. Then he opened a box that sparkled with treasure, with a stack of small metal rings. He pinched one out with the tips of his fingers and placed it into the teeth of some pliers. He took the bird once more from its sack, holding it still in the light-firm grasp she had seen him using before. He turned the creature onto its back, extending its left leg out with his thumb, with a touch that was softer than sound. His awkward left hand lifted the pliers and brought them over the leg. He squeezed the head of the instrument firm. The bird looked round with curious indifference; a metal ring clipped to its leg. He inspected the bird once again. He stroked its head with the edge of his knuckle, as if to calm it, as if to caress it. As if unwilling to let it go free. Then he brought it up towards the window; he held it out through the crack. For an instant, both bird and man were as one. He opened his hands. His palms fell away. It was gone.

Without pause, he picked up a second sack. This bird was smaller than the last they had seen. Its upper parts were warm brown feathers; its underside a creamy buff; the tips of its wing and tail deep brown; its eyebrow almost pure white. The girl sat mute beside the man – tirelessly watching him, watching the bird, watching them both as they came together: sharing the same sudden-startled movement, sharing the same steady stare. Here was a wild thing prised from the wild, captured in mid-flight whilst skidding the reeds, plucked out of nothing by intricate fingers, put in a sack, raised, held and measured, then freed once more to the wild.

The girl watched, enchanted by all that she saw, by the ritual unfolding before her. It seemed unnatural to be catching the birds; yet the way they were captured, the way they were freed, felt completely natural and fair. Both of these feelings engrossed her entirely, confused and entwined in her raptured subconscious, perfect and senseless and whole. She dared not talk, nor dared she to breathe, in case the man should see she was here, for fear he sent her away. She wanted only to watch, and to witness. To guess at the shape, the colour, the size of those birds that still danced in their sacks. To watch as each was held and caressed; to watch as each was turned in his hands; to watch at that instant each stood in his palms; to watch as each opened its wings and was gone.

The man had opened the fourth white sack. When he reached to the bench to pick up the ruler, she pressed it into his palm. She did the same with the scales. When he sought his pliers, she gave them to him already primed with a ring. He made no comment, but he took them from her, handing them back when not needed. When the final bird had escaped through the window, he removed his tools and replaced the book on its shelf.

Outside, the day was bright and pale. The sun had risen, though it hid beyond a bulbous buffer of cloud. The air was clear; there was no morning mist. The wind was tame; it was teasing the reeds to twirl their tassels while swirling together, delighting in being alive. In silence, they stepped out and strode up the track. She sensed no urgency now. The girl watched the man looking over the ley. She knew he was watching his nets. She felt she had also started to know them, just as she knew of the openings and paths, of the trails that led to its heart.

One final time they came down the track, inspecting the nets from the fringe of the reeds. At the hut they collected their rain-damp jackets, then made their way to the dune. The sun was melting the clouds with its heat as they parted to go separate ways. As she watched him depart, she could feel its warmth stroking a fondness over her shoulders, stealing into her skin.

In the days that followed, the girl became an inseparable part of the man's routine. She entered his world imperceptibly, so he couldn't see how far she had come, or how close she became to that world. She came with such a spotless simplicity he couldn't object, he couldn't deny, even should he have wanted. At first, it was just the slightest of touches – handing him sacks when they stood by the nets, loading his pliers with a ring. She noticed all the things he found awkward, all that burdened his weak left arm. Her observation was fine and acute; her remedy being herself. She was nimble-fingered and had keen quick eyes. She could mend the bridges of bended reed; she could pick through tangles that fouled his nets; she could walk with a string of sacks on a stick as she followed him back to the hut. And, in time, she attended his book, she entered the records in a neat round hand, as he called them out, each in turn. And all the while, she acted true – both to him and herself. No more did she trip on the bridges of reed, nor fail to keep pace, nor fail to stay still, as she stood entranced by the man.

Why do you write all these notes?
To track the birds and see how they live. You can't do that simply by watching.
Doesn't it hurt them to be trapped?

No. The net doesn't hurt them.

How do you know? Can't birds feel pain?

All animals are able to feel pain. It's instinctive. They might not process it like us. But they can feel it the same.

Doesn't the ring hurt them?

No. It's very light. They don't really notice the weight.

What does it say on the ring?

There's a reference number. If the bird's caught again, we can track it back to when and where it was caught. That way we build up a living picture of where it's been and how long it's lived. We can track it for all of its life.

Are you likely to catch the same bird again?

Maybe not me. But there are hundreds of people all over England – all over the world – who keep track. One in fifty is caught again. That's thousands of birds every year.

But I still don't see why we need to catch them. Why can't we let them be free?

As days rolled by, she began to see why. And sight led a path into knowledge. Into understanding his motivation. Into understanding herself. Reasons too deep, too complex for words; reasons which lingered like fierce-rooted secrets far from the surface of thought. Reasons that only in actions and motions crept into the conscious and laid themselves bare. For him, it was the knowledge, the learning, the birds, and the wanting to be as a bird. For her, it was more. It was all that, and more. The freedom of morning; the cold on her cheek; the smell of the earth; the sound of the sky; the surprise of the sea as it rolled in towards them, as it whispered its welcome in the first blush of dawn. Nature was coming to life all around her. A nature boundless, released. That was her reason; that was her all. That was her purpose. Her life.

The girl was learning a different language, she was learning a whole different world. One of colours and motions and calls; of senses and feelings and sound. She could tell the bunting by its bright collar. The bearded reedling by its call. The sedge warbler by its creamy belly. The reed warbler by its grating song. The yellow wagtail by its dance – spreading its tail and plumping its feathers, shivering the tips of its wings. The meadow pipit by its grey-speckled breast, as it fluttered far above the ley, as it glided back towards the reeds, singing aloud while descending. Sometimes they trapped a rarer bird – a tawny pipit, a Cetti's warbler – and the man would smile for having no words, with a childlike joy he couldn't contain. At other times they came upon a bird that was already ringed. Then the measureless world that the two of them peopled was shocked by the pleasure he felt.

Each morning, early, they set out from the dune, inspecting the nets on this side of the ley. Sometimes they found a half-dozen birds – trapped, forlorn – in a single net, piping the sound of freedom lost. At other times, the same net stood idle, blowing emptily for days in the wind. There was no knowing, no way of knowing, no reason why it was so. She stood at the man's side, holding the sacks, not daring to touch the birds themselves, though wanting them to be free. Once all the nets had been seen and inspected, they returned to the hut with their spoils. It was all bare boards; it was barren and airless; it was damp, stale-smelling and cold. But when harbouring six or ten sacks full of birds, it was rampant with music, with life. Here in the hut was nature itself, caught for a time but still wild. Here they had captured the heart of the ley. Here its soul was laid bare.

In the early evening, they made their way to the other side of the ley. He showed her a path which wound through the reeds, which spanned the full breadth of their bed. It began as the others, cut over the streams, until it came to a plank. Here was the widest, darkest channel, scythed through the core of the ley. The brackish water gushed beneath it, and when swollen the plank was submerged. The stream itself was eight feet wide, and when first she had seen it, she had taken fright. She had pictured the stream, and herself within it, staring up from its depths. Though now, accompanied by the man, she dared not register fear. She shuffled sideways down the plank, balancing with her arms outstretched, watching the water spinning beneath her, luring her into its deeps. Once over the river, the path led on, weaving its course amidst the reeds till it landed on the far bank.

She looked back. She had crossed the ley; she had walked on water. Over the tips of the whispering tassels, she could see the field, the snug of the farmhouse, a world away from her own.

This farther side of the ley was unknown. She had never dared to cross it before. She followed close in the tracks that he made, treading with care in his footprints. There were nets here too, and beside the nets was another hut hidden by scrub. This cabin was bigger, and more robust. It backed into the bank and was sheltered by bushes, its floor raised up on short stilts. There were four steps up to the door. As with the other, this hut was bare, with a table running the length of the wall, a wooden bench, and a long, low window. But, unlike the other, the principal chamber opened into a second room, with a wider bench which might act as a bed, and a rug spread over the floor.

From this larger hut they made for the beach. From here they could cross the ley at its neck, they could wade through the water, ankle-deep, as it wound its way to the sea. Approaching the dune in the glum of the dusk, the girl stopped and called to the man –

Look! There's an otter.
That's not an otter. It's too small. It's a mink.
A mink? I didn't think mink could live in this country.
They do. They were brought over from America. They escaped and then became wild. They eat birds. They raid their nests searching for eggs. Look what colour it is.
Yes. I can see it. It's brown.
It's dark brown. And the hair is more glossy. Otters are bigger and lighter brown. An otter's eyes are high on its head, so it can see around it when swimming.
What sort of an animal is an otter?
It's a large type of weasel. Weasels are vicious. They can climb trees and scrabble down holes. They raid birds' nests and they kill the chicks. They are ravenous eaters, and they have no fear.
Don't you like any animals except birds?
I like badgers. They don't ever eat birds. Except perhaps for dead ones. I feel sorry for them, too. We kill them.
We don't mean to kill them. Not on purpose.
Yes, we do. Farmers fear they spread disease, so they are systematically killed. And besides that, their own world is shrinking. There isn't any room for the wild anymore. It's only here – or in places like this – they can dare to be free. But even here it's not safe.
Are people really that nasty? Is there no one you like?
I try to like people. I think I like some. I like you.

Between the dawn and the dusk, the rain and the sun, the capture and the release of the birds, he told her all that he knew. Everything he had learnt of the ley; all she desired or could dream of learning. He told her about the harvest mouse, with its tail which wound itself round the reeds as it anchored itself in the wind. He told her about the secretive wood mouse, and where it stored food, and how it sat up and washed itself when surprised. He told her all he knew about rabbits, about rats and squirrels and voles. He told her about the species of deer, about snakes and foxes and moles. About kestrels and buzzards and kites and owls. About all on the land, and all in the air. She sapped the man of all he knew. She drained him of his years in the ley in those few fierce summer days.

Dawn. Daybreak. Morning. Noon. Slow afternoon. The gradual evening. Twilight. Dusk. Darkness. Night. All day the girl was near the ley. But in the fringes of the day the ley became her world. Then she became as much of it as every creature round her. Now hers a land of hinter-light – of sunless, starless endless skies which switched from black, to gold, to grey. A universe where time was void of any meaning, any sense. Where all collapsed into the now. Where all was free to be itself, to live – ubiquitous, entire – detached from that which lay beyond: the fields that stood about its fringe, the world of people farther still. She lived this glorious wilderness, this empire built on frail foundations, neither land nor sea. By day she breathed, by night she dreamt it. The ley pulsated round her veins. It terrorised her mind. She lived it ineluctably. Utterly devoted in and through and with and for it. All of it was part of her, and everything she knew within it. And she the essence of its being; she the substance of it all.

The man adored the birds. He lived for them; they gave him life. The girl adored them too. But on their own they weren't enough, however beautiful they were. She lived for something more. For something they were just a part of, something more complete. A sense, a fact, a certainty. Absolute and all-consuming, all bound up within the now. An ageless, timeless entity. A purity beyond all doubt, beyond all blot or sin or stain. A clarity, an innocence; a perfect and exquisite truth. The glory of the ley.

The Treason

The summer days were growing long; the evenings drawing in and shorter; the mornings cold and dark. The girl looked out across the ley; she knew the meaning of these signs. Though she had come to measure time in fractions of eternity, within a single day which dawned repeatedly and never closed, she knew that time was passing still. Out there, in that so distant world – one peopled by humanity. Where time was measured by the clock; where time moved on in linear paths, which never turned back on themselves. Where this diurnal natural cycle sank beneath the weight of man. Where it was crushed beneath his claw. A world apart from hers.

Her world was all the ley. It had become her single truth, entire and absolute. The ley was all she ever needed, all she knew or cared for. And yet she knew that other world would come and try to steal her back. She knew for certain it would come. This confidence she kept a secret, even from herself. Though it would sometimes interfere – within a nightmare, in a phone call, in a letter through the post – intruding, mocking, ravaging her perfect world, her bliss. She could not contemplate the thought of being taken back to London. She could not think nor yet believe that she could ever leave. The girl was bonded to the ley with ties more fixed than blood or stone. She fused to it, inseparable. Its paramour, its bleeding heart; its sacrifice, its bride.

Each day, she rose before the dawn. She dressed and tripped the misted field. She reached the dune before the sun – watching as it shred the dark, waiting for the man.

Every day it was the same. The same, and always new. Ever never quite complete. Today, again, the same.

They nodded their silence and strolled down the track. Together they entered the hut. They picked up their bags and slipped down to the reeds, walking within them as though upon land: knowing each footfall, each contour, each bridge, with the untutored knowing of being. They worked the nets in harmony, their four hands born of a single body, releasing and bagging the captured birds in a single effortless wave. Together they looked out onto the reeds, alerting the other by intuition; enriching, fulfilling the other's gaze. Together they went back into the hut, passing the tools between themselves unconsciously and in perfect silence, in a seamless fluid unified movement. They thought and worked and were as one being. Existing in a place beyond thinking. Here there was only the being, the living. The moment was all, and they shared it between them. The whole world, the fullness and richness of feeling, wrapped in an infinite now.

Sometimes she felt – when sat in the tree awaiting the dusk, when stood on the dune awaiting the dawn – that she should give something back to the man. She wanted to thank him, to show her thanks, to share with him in return. Yet nothing was wanted. His was such simplicity that it fed off only the little he needed, and that little he found in the ley. There was nothing beside it for him. She couldn't imagine him living beyond, nor how he survived when outside. There was nothing to give from that world that he wanted, nothing to give that she had. All she could give was a gift from the ley. All she could give was herself. She and the ley were a single being – the totality of all that was living – the only thing she could share.

The evening was thawing and rich, with a warmth that stole through the skin. Under the slightest whisper of breeze, the sweating reeds fretted and tossed. It was too warm for the birds; too warm to be moving. The sky was huge and stretched across the immensity of her sight. A tapestry woven from blue and gold thread, burnished and blushing and bleeding its beauty. The girl lay on her back on the cushioning dune, watching it, feeling it washing within her, drawing it in with each breath.

The man came up from the beach. He nodded, and they went together down the dune and onto the track. They inspected the nets on the nearer side, though knowing that nothing would be there. The day was still too lazy, too light. They walked to the path which led through the ley, they sliced through the reeds at the very same place where – weeks before, and whole lifetimes ago – the girl had scattered her stones. The bridges sighed beneath their feet; the tassels lisped their faint lies.

As she came to the broad channel spanned by the plank, a shape in the water caught her eye. At first, she thought it was merely a branch, sticking partially out of the stream. It was greenish-grey, and was dotted with spots. Though, as she watched, she could see it was moving. Its body slowly, deliberately sinking. Its head still standing proud of the water. Its glazed eyes fixed and unblinking.

Then it flexed its muscular form; it was gone.

Did you see that?
Yes. That was a grass snake.
Can they swim?

Yes. They're very good swimmers. They usually swim with their heads above water. But they can stay underwater for ages too. That's where they catch all their food. They swallow their victims alive.

What do they eat?

Frogs, toads, fish. Sometimes mice or birds.

So you don't like them?

No. But they're strange animals. When they're threatened they're able to puff up their bodies to make them look bigger and scary. If you touch them, a smelly liquid comes out. Sometimes they also play dead. They roll onto their backs and stay very still. Their mouths open, their tongues hanging out.

But they're not dangerous?

They have some venom, but they're harmless to humans.

Are there any other snakes in the ley?

No. Not snakes. There are slow worms, though. They look like snakes, but they aren't. They're really lizards without any legs. You can tell a snake because it doesn't have eyelids. A snake isn't able to blink.

The girl raised her eyes to look at the man. He was here; he was standing before her. Here, in the reeds, in the heart of the ley. Deep in their magical world. Their world. She watched his lips as he spoke. His sentences were all stabbed and staccato; the words stammered out and spoken to her. To no one other than her. Why should he open this secretive world and choose to share it with her? He was standing before her and talking to her, his awkward eyes restless, assessing their world without ever resting on hers. His poorly arm hung by his side. Why did he share his passion with her? Why did he want to reveal its enigmas and let her see into its truth?

The girl let his words fall away. She let them wash on the wind unheard. She saw only the fragile fidgety man, framed in the majesty of a sky livid and singed with molten sun, encircled by a ring of harsh reed bent in homage and pain. He alone, in this absolute world. Lord and conjurer of it all. He who knew all; who brought it to life; who shared it and gave life to her.

And, in that instant, that moment of joy, the girl leant forward and hugged him.

The next morning was colourless. Earth, sea, sky were all washed out; they were drained and draped in drab greyness. The world lay bare, unsharpened, unformed; seemingly to lack all motion and life; prone and cool in a film of thin mist, awaiting the touch of the dawn. The girl sat on the shadowed dune, sensing its emptiness. It was all so familiar, so alien. It was beautiful, magical, hateful, complete. It owned her, it possessed her entirely. She could only submit to its splendour. She watched the sky as it splintered to life; the crest of the sun behind the hills drawing them darker into themselves before melting them soft in its light. She watched the reeds as they welcomed the dawn, lisping a eulogy, murmuring prayer.

The girl knew by the light, by the wind, by the sea, that by now the man should be here. But he wasn't – not here on the dune. If not here, he was already working the nets. He, who was also born of the ley; he, who was part of the whole. A part of its intricate chain of life; the heart that hid at its core. She knew he was here; he couldn't escape.

125

The girl slipped from the dune and onto the track, walking as he would, tracing his steps. She took to the path that led to the ruin, reaching its rambling outline of stone without sight or sound of the man. Then she mirrored his movement and started back, searching attentively over the reeds, listening into their whispering chorus, seeking amidst their splaying tips for a sign that the man was within. She stood outside the mouths of each entrance, her head bent low, her ear to the tassels, as if they would share their knowledge with her. She retraced her path down the track. And there, approaching a route through their midst, she saw an irregular shiver of reeds, slicing a single soundless path further into the ley.

She pressed through the scrub till she reached the entrance, thrusting her rude hands forwards and outwards, parting the reeds and revealing a path. She entered, stepping more slowly than usual across the crisp bridges that structured the ley. She stopped in a patch of whispering reeds, wanting to eavesdrop in on their chant. She took ten more steps, then squat on her haunches. She peered through the thin wall of rushes before her.

Through the wall she could see him – she could see his shadow – vague and distorted, and blown like the reeds towards the heart of the ley. She could see his right hand plucking a net. She could see him reach for a sack from his bag. She could see him shuffling slowly sideways, inspecting every inch of the web, touching it tenderly, smooth as a skin, utterly caught in his task.

When the man had reached the end of the net, he came through a gap in the wall. The girl stood up, only three feet before him, stood on the path which led to the bank.

He said nothing. For an instant only she recognised a seeming shock of surprise in his eyes, in the mask of his passionless face. Then he stepped around her and struck down the path. She turned, before doing the same.

She followed, two paces behind him. His face was obscured and he didn't look round. They continued their journey together alone. As they came to another path through the reeds, the man dipped off to one side. Again, she followed behind him. Over plump bridges; down the bone path. When he stopped at the net, she stood by his side. Ready and wanting to help him. A stray bullfinch was entwined in the mesh, caught almost upside down. The man raised his right arm up to the web, his fingers like spindles, fast and precise, working the netting round and through till the twisted wings were set free. Then he released the feathery neck. And all the while, he was holding and stroking – he was cradling the startled body – so the bird experienced no fear. As his clumsy left hand reached for a sack, the girl thrust one into his palm. And again, once the bird was safely within, she reached out and tied the sack to his bag. With no words; no glance; no expression. All reliant on instinct. They returned to the track, retracing their steps, until they came to the hut.

The man opened the door and went in. He placed his bag on the edge of the bench, dangling the six white sacks that it held. He took his implements from the shelf; he sat down and opened his book. The girl sat down too. As his hand reached out towards a sack, her arm slid over and guided the book back to where she was sitting. He opened the sack, his right hand blind, gently feeling and seeing inside. And now, his hand and the head of a bird emerged – flushed and fabulous – into bewildering day.

The girl gave him a ruler to measure the wingspan. She glanced at the man's hands, noting its length, and recorded the span in her book. Effortlessly, she swapped the ruler back for a sack, watching the bird submerge in its folds, then handing the scales to the man. The small barrel bounced to an even weight which she entered into a column. The bird looked on, incredulous, squinting and twitching and calm. She passed the man the pair of pliers, already loaded and fixed with a ring. She noted its number against the same entry as his blunt hand closed on the grip. Without raising his eyes, the man muttered one word, as light and as thin as the wind in the room. She caught it and wrote the numerals down in the last empty column along the same row, recording the age of the bird.

And now, invisible, she continued to watch, as he took the elegant bird in his hand, as its head caressed the edge of his knuckle, as he brought it over and into the light, as it smelt the air and it tasted freedom, as he let his palms fall away to the bench, as it sat unsupported in air for an instant, as he urged it to life, as it shook its head and opened its wings, as it kicked its feet and was gone.

Again, they repeated the identical task. And then again, rehearsed once again, till all six birds were set free.

He replaced the book and the tools on the shelf. He crossed the room and left the hut. He stood in the clearing, in a pale pool of sedge, looking up at the sky. It was faceless and grey; not light nor dark, not breaking nor threatening rain. The air was cool and still. Dew clung to the grass, the bushes, the thorn. He walked through the scrub and up to the track. Then he stopped.

She saw him hesitate. Here was the entrance to the path that led to the farther side of the ley. There were two more nets that had yet to be checked. The day was late in coming to being. The ley was still feverish with life.

She knew he knew they should cut through the reeds; they should go to inspect the remaining nets. In that moment, he almost looked at her, as if he had heard her thinking his thoughts. As if he recalled, in that fraction of being, who she was, and why she was there. For the first time that day – as if for a first time – as if, in that flicker, he cared. Just for an instant. An instant that was already dying; that was already part of the past and was lost.

Now she watched as he stood undecided, at half-angles both to the track and the path which wound its way through the ley. His body was static as he fought for direction, as she hadn't seen him before. She watched, and she waited for him to choose. Whatever he wanted; whatever was right. The man looked up to the sky once more, clouded and blinded and bulging with shame. Then he turned down the bank, he parted the reeds, he entered the ley and was gone.

The girl followed him with her eyes. She saw the reeds give way before him; she saw them close and take him in. She saw them bend as he moved down the path – reed after reed which bowed before him. She projected an imaginary line in her mind: she pictured the route which led to the plank that lay over the stream that cut through its heart, then over more bridges and onwards. On, to the farther side. To the track and the hill which stretched to the sky; to the hedges stitched to the land like its seams. And between them, the ley, her reason to be.

Now she could see him no more.

The girl went down to the reeds. She eased them apart with her hands. And without the need to look down at her feet, she followed the route that the man had taken, closing herself in its shade.

She found him again by a net. She came so soft, so soundlessly, he was only aware that she was there when she reached out and gave him a sack. He took it from her without a pause. Without a murmur, a look. A meadow pipit and a small goldcrest were tangled up in the web. The man raised his right hand up to the gauze, plucking both birds from the off-balanced net. Then he stepped down the path and out of the reeds, retracing the track which led to the hut, stepping slow in the cool of the air.

Again, at the steps of the hut, he stopped. She saw him hesitate, as though at a loss. Almost as though the door was locked, and he realised he hadn't a key. He stood on the top step, frozen in motion, his whole face void of any emotion, his hand half-held to the handle. She could hear the reeds as they chattered together, whispering secrets in mystical language, nodding a knowingness known only to them. The sedge to the man's side was bristling and trembling, seeming to snatch out and clutch at the hut. The two white sacks that hung to his side danced randomly in a fierce tiny frenzy. Their tugs at his bag brought him back to his sense. He reached for the handle and opened the door. Again, and as ever and always before, she followed him into the hut.

Inside, she took their tools from the shelf, laying them down to the side of the book. He placed his bag on the edge of the table, allowing the sacks to hang in the air.

Then they sat to examine their prize. He reached for a bird, removing its covering, catching it up in the thrill of his hand, between his fingers and thumb. He took the ruler held out before him. Then the scales; then the pliers. He breathed a number into the air, in the barren room where they sat. She wrote as he spoke, in clear bold letters. And now the record was done. He took the bird and stroked its head with the edge of his knuckle, side on. He brought it up towards the window, letting his palms drop, falling away, so the creature was able to fly.

The man reached out for the second sack, and they took to the task once more – repeating each step deliberately, with a fixed, a quiet intent. The girl bent over the busy book, till every column was filled. When she looked up, ready to pack away, she saw they were not yet done. They must have caught three birds, not two. For there was another white sack still to come – it was lying flat in his lap. Through the cloth she could make out the bulge of a body; she could see something moving inside.

She waited, expecting the man to release it. But he made no attempt to remove the sack. He sat still, just watching it twitch. Outside, the sky was deadened and grey, dull and shapeless and lacking all form. The air was still; the reeds were soundless; the ley was holding its breath. She knew the creature must be released; it had to be taken out and set free. If he wouldn't do it, she must. Perhaps that was why he had left it. As a test, as a gift, as a means of proving all she had learned from the man. And she wanted to show him all she had learned. She ached to show him she could. That she had acquired the knowing from him, the tenderness of his touch. That she was ready to hold a creature, firm and safe in her grasp.

Just as she had seen him do, every morning since that first morning, she placed one hand around the sack, holding it steady while loosening its strings. She reached inside with care, feeling through the threaded folds till she felt the creature itself. Here, in her grasp, its blunted head peeping out of her fist. Then she let the sack fall away to the floor, and there it was, taut and aggressive – muscular – caught in the firm of her hand. She held it steady, not wanting to shock it, feeling the urgent pulse of its blood beat through its blinded body.

The girl took the ruler from the bench to measure the creature's length. She placed the hook of the scale round its neck, attempting to fathom its weight. But she did no more, for having no legs there was nowhere for her to fasten a ring. The girl opened her palms and let her hands drop, hoping the creature would fly. But instead, it slumped back into his lap, and lay there snarled in a tangled nest, twitching and vomiting, bloated and pink.

The girl reached out for her book. She took up the pen intending to write. Then she paused. Her measurements had proven futile; there was nothing she could record. She closed the book, she took up the tools, she placed them all on the shelf. When she had finished, she turned around. She saw that the creature had gone. Only the man was there, staring at nothing; not looking, nor moving, nor speaking. Through the window, the day was coming alive. She could see from its shape it was starting to form; it was starting to take its first vital breaths. A silver morning was slowly unfurling – the green fields vibrant, kissed by the breeze, the reeds ecstatic with light. So bright, so brilliant, so wide. She knew their trapping was done for the day.

The girl stood up and left the hut. She closed the door behind her.

The day was still in its infancy. The sun was fierce in her eyes, on her skin. It danced on her face and her neck. But it didn't caress. It felt intrusive and stung with wet heat. Without warning, she found she had leapt from the steps, she had started to run away from the hut, she had started to run down the track. She ran away from the bushes and scrub, towards the sun and the sea. Running still faster – urgently fast – till she couldn't see the scratch of the grass as it skidded under her feet. She hurled herself up and over the dune; she savagely pulled at her clothes. She plunged her body into the sea. She thrashed at the frothing gurgling water, feeling its chill as it slapped at her face, as it prickled and snatched at her limbs.

She stopped swimming; she turned towards land. She saw an open stretch of water, broad and brimming with effervescence, with white-spumed wavelets haloed in gold, spread in a shimmering sheen of raw beauty. And beyond it, she saw the line of the beach, the less distinct slope of the dune.

She had swum a long distance out. She had never swum this far before. She stretched her feet in a watery tiptoe, feeling nothing beneath her but sea. Feeling nothing. Numb to all feeling. She paddled her hands, turning seawards once more. A breeze was teasing the waves. It seemed to toy with the vast reach of water that was rolling towards her – the silver-grey ripples that played at her chin, the miniature breakers that splashed on her cheek. The huge ocean stretched out before her.

She shivered.

She lay her head back on the pillow of water. She kicked out her feet and arched her back till the crown of her tummy broke through the surge. She stopped breathing and let her eyes close. She could feel, she could feel herself clenched in tight stasis, even whilst caught in the constant motion – rising and falling with each gentle swell, reflecting the wash of the sea. She felt touched by the water, held and caressed. Every inch of her being, her supine body, supported and swathed in its strength. It was endlessly fluid, it was almost solid – so completely it held her, without seeming effort, in an infinite, perfect embrace. She could taste its rude salt as it stung at her mouth, she could feel it dissolved in the water around her, she could feel it matting her hair. She felt herself drifting, moving through being, carried along in a careless current, further and further away. She felt herself borne by it, melding within it, becoming a part of its rhythm and sway. It was clutching her to it, it was cleansing her soul, it was washing her, washing all feeling away. She looked through the close of her tight-clenched eyelids, and saw a spread of golden red, a purity of blind sight.

In time she heard another noise that was building steadily to her side. At first, it seemed no more than a whisper, a distant shiver; though it grew ever louder, till it slapped in her ears. The girl rolled over, treading the water, daring to open her eyes. The sound was the sea on the rocks nearby. The stealthy current had borne her away, almost the length of the beach. Now she was locked in the shadow of cliffs. She swam swiftly back to the shore. She ran back to her pile of sun-warmed clothes, pulling them on and feeling them pinch at her still-wet, sea-stained flesh.

The sun had broken the palette of sky and was leaning harsh on her back. She walked along the firm wet sand, beside the ever-retreating waves and their endless, breathless exhale. For days, in her mind, she had pictured herself putting her hand inside a sack, feeling the soft of a bird's warm feathers, easing its wing from its delicate frame, clutching its urgent body close, holding it for an immeasurable instant – there on the flat of her outstretched palm – watching it fluttering and flying away. That was how she thought it would be. A sensation of utter delight. The man had let her open a sack, it was true. But it wasn't the creature she thought. He had given her something bald and angry; a thing that could neither fly nor walk; a thing that coughed in livid convulsions whilst fettered and fixed in its nest. A thing that could puff up its stunted body, that could shoot its venom into her hand. He had told her about it once before.

He had let her handle a snake.

The girl had come to the end of the beach. Instead of turning back to the farm, she continued up the winding path, between the sedge, the gorse and the grass which grew on the shoulders of a cliff and led to the brow of a hill. Before her, she saw an unspoilt valley, a different beach, a new sea. And an infinity of glorious sky.

The girl climbed down to the rocks. She stepped over chains that were strapped in the sand, that tethered small vessels and buoys. She skirted the ramp which led from a boathouse; she slipped up a slope at the end of the beach to enter a sheltering wood. She followed a path that spun through the trees. It felt close and cold in its cheerless insides. The dampened floor was scattered with twigs.

At the farther end of the wood, she came to acres of curling bracken that stretched inland from the cliff. She waded through its blinding carpet, dragging her feet through its stems. Beyond the bracken were pools of gorse, and farther still was the stump of a headland. The girl steered a slanting path towards it, scrambling over dry-stone walls, scrabbling up a sheet of rock, determined to scale to the top. To both sides of the promontory was the sea, and in front of her too, though obscured by the crest of the hill. The final ascent had grown steep. She climbed and crawled through the spongy grass, pulling her body up by her hands.

As her head and shoulders came over the summit a barrage of wind exploded about her, tearing her jacket and forcing her back. She recoiled before trying again. And this time, instead of seeking to stand, she slunk on her stomach, anchoring herself to the ground with her heels and her hands. Her windward side was shocked by the blast, her cheek on fire, her eardrum pummelled by the unrelenting turmoil of wind. Turning her head, she glanced at the sea, cut with white horses and churning in hollows, brilliant with light and roaring its glory. She rolled back below the line of the squall, faint with exhaustion, shielding her face from the buffeting wind.

Ten. Twenty. Thirty.

She rolled onto the summit once more. Again, she could feel the sting of the salt that was spitting into her skin; she could feel the wind skewering into her side. She turned her head to look it full on: locking her jaw and squinting her eyes at the sheer ferocity of the sea. At its bellowing majesty.

Ten. Twenty. Thirty.

Then down, back down to her hollow. She shivered. She could feel the wet of sweat on her back. She could feel that wetness turning cold. She hunched her shoulders, stretching her shirt across the slick of her trembling skin – absorbing the moisture, hugging her warmth, stealing the heat of her body.

Ten. Twenty. Thirty.

Then, once again, to the crest. Now she was looking straight down the cliff – down at the curling, circling waves – watching the swell and the crack of impact as the water crashed on the rock. Again and again. Remorseless.

Thirty.

She rolled from the summit a final time, her body in free fall, tumbling out of control, till she came to rest in a patch of tall grass. She lay with her eyes closed, hid from the wind, hid from the heat of the sun. Beneath the endless empty sky, she lay inert and sucked in the silence, hearing it heaving around her.

When she was ready, she arose. She marched away from the windswept headland, skirting below the line of the cliff on sheltered paths which wound through the wasteland crouched beneath its fierce brow. She walked on into another valley, where a large pipe sprung from a concrete base and spewed water into the sea. She mirrored the contours of the cliff, climbing up the side of a hill, then falling and sliding away with the land towards a bleak muddy estuary. She slithered down splintered shards of rock, through pools of seaweed and transparent shrimps, till she stood alongside the river.

A stretch of deserted virgin sand spread wide on the other side of the water. She could feel it calling to her. If you can cross, then you will be free. Free forever more. She came to the river's edge. It cut through the sand and was ten feet wide, shelving down to a depthless brown.

The girl took off her socks and her shoes. She took off her trousers and pants. She rolled her dress and her top up high, clamping them under her arm. She bundled her clothes and held them above her; she slipped cautiously down the soft shelf of sand till up to her knees in the cool rapid stream. She could feel the current pull at her legs, sucking hard at her skin. She took a single step back.

Free forever. Forever.

She looked at the stretch of unsullied sand; she looked at the river once more. Silvery goose-pimples puckered her skin and stood proud on her glistening legs. She took a hesitant half-step forward; then another, now more assured. The water was gurgling round her thighs, bubbling as it met with her flesh, giggling, seeming delighted. She wanted to balance herself with a stick; to put out a hand to steady herself; to have something solid to hold. Two more shuffled steps. And now she was in the heart of the river, with the water up to her ribs.

Forever. Forever.

She should go back. She knew she ought to return. She took a half-step forwards once more, sinking down further and wetting her dress. She drew back her foot in alarm. She shouldn't be in a river like this. She knew that she shouldn't be here. She edged upstream by scuffling sideways, stabilising her unsteady body by splaying her arms and her legs. She could feel the water ripping her sides, weighing into her flank, as if it knew how precarious she was, how close to falling and sinking. If only the pressure would cease for an instant. Just for a moment; just now. She sensed how low she was in the water; how close it had come to her neck. This wasn't the same as the sea. This wasn't intent on buoying her up. This only wanted to suck her down; to drown and bury her in its blind depths. To bury her in its scorn. Her arms were heavy above her head. Her legs were sluggish and quivering with fear. With weariness and the shame.

Free forever. Forever free.

She looked up, squinting towards the sun, absorbing its warmth and its strength. She scuffed her right foot upstream. Then forwards. She dragged her legs against the pressure, digging her toes in the sand. And this time she felt the shelving depths lean ever so slightly back up. She caught her breath. Two more quick steps. Now thigh deep, and the current was less. She was almost dancing, almost walking on water. Even now, she was here on the sand. And now she was laughing, like the river was laughing. Both of them laughing. Both here and now, and both together. Both of them free forever.

There, on the farther side of the river, the sun and the wind came together and dried her. Then she went to the fringe of the sea. And there, in huge letters, she wrote her name in the sand. When she finished, she went and sat on some rocks. And there she sat – she sat forever – she sat till the tide turned and swallowed her name. Till the water washed her away. Till she knew and truly knew in her heart that now at last she was free. She was free.

When next she looked up, the day was gone. Effaced and expunged from her sight. The river, the beach, the sweep of sand. All of it gone, all lost and erased, as if it had never existed. As if it were part of a different realm, of a life that was lived before now. Of a distant time, remote in the past, when she was a ten-year-old girl. So long ago it scarcely seemed real; she no longer seemed who she was. That time in the past, and who she was then, no more than a fiction, a lie.

Instead of the beach and the sand and the sea, there were fields and hedges and whispers of sedge. And she was no longer sitting and watching – she was walking fast through the snatching grass, her head bent, her eyes to the ground.

The girl looked up. Evening was closing swiftly around her. A partial darkness, uncoloured and hard, hung on the eastern horizon. It was draining the land and all within it, dissolving all semblance of matter. She could see she was crossing the heart of a field. She knew that field to be hers. The last strands of tentative daylight were withering and stubbing themselves in the sea. The random shapes of cows were emerging, floating on an indistinct ocean. Then the loom of the farmhouse, sombre above her. And she, a stranger, walking towards it. She came to the gate, and climbed its bars –

Ha!

The girl screamed. She fell from the gate, and into the yard. Into the yard. And now she was rolling onto her feet. Onto her feet, running into the house. Running inside, and straight to her room. She was pushing her bed against the door, closing the window, tugging the blinds.

She was sinking down, her back to the wall, hugging her knees in her arms. Her face hot and heavy with tears.

Slowly, sensation returned. She could hear a noise from outside. She could hear someone enter the house from the yard. She could make out the sound of a person talking, though she couldn't capture the words.

There was a knock on her door. The handle was tried. Then someone was calling to her. A voice that she knew. The voice of her aunt. It was her aunt who was speaking to her. She said that she hadn't meant to scare her. She had only just finished the evening feed. She had called out simply to say hello. She hadn't expected to shock her. Would the girl like to come out and have some supper? The kitchen was warming and bright. The table was laid. The dogs and the cat were all wanting to see her; they had been wanting to see her all day.

Silence. More words. More silence.

The aunt stood still on the farther side, waiting and hoping and waiting. But the girl didn't reply, she didn't come out. She stayed in the darkness; she stayed in her room. She stayed with her back pressed up to the wall, clasping her knees to her chest.

At dawn, the girl didn't go to the ley. Nor did she help with the morning feed. She rose late; she crept to the kitchen to eat; she slipped outside to the Judas tree. All morning the girl hid high in its branches, obscured in the depths of its shivering leaves. At the height of the day, beyond those leaves, she heard her aunt calling to her. At the base of the trunk, she could see she was standing, inviting her down to have lunch.

The girl closed her ears and turned away. She switched her gaze to the ley. She emptied her mind of all else. She stared and she stared at the distant reeds, moving as one, as a single mass, soundless and fluid and graceful. She stretched her opened arms towards them, as if to draw them into her chest. As though she was wanting to bridge the divide, to dive through the leaves and float through the air, till safe in the body of ley. She was reaching towards it, yearning for it; yet all she could feel was a rupture of distance, an invisible barrier which seemed to have grown and risen between them, holding it further away. She was trapped in her tree, she was caught in its web, and nothing and no one was there to release her. Not even her aunt – her sentinel – who stood in the glum of its shadows. Reluctantly, she climbed down the trunk. She met with her aunt in the shifting shade –

Do you want to talk about yesterday?
No.
Why didn't you go to the ley today?
I didn't want to.
I found Flasher's cage in the bin. Is he all right?
Flasher's dead.
O, I'm so sorry. What happened?
He had an accident.
What sort of an accident?
He got caught between the bars. He crushed his skull.
He crushed himself?
Yes.
I didn't think animals could do that.
Well, he did.
Really?

Yes.

Shall we keep the cage? You might want to get another.

I won't.

I thought you liked animals.

I don't.

Since when?

I don't like things with feathers or fur. They're smelly and dirty.

No, they're not.

I might get a snake.

A snake?

I think a snake would be good.

Why?

It hasn't got any fur. You can feel its skin. The skin of a living thing.

I don't think I'd like to have a snake as a pet.

You're not me.

No, I'm not.

That afternoon she buried Flasher. He was placed in a wooden pencil box, with the lid slid over his shame. Just for an instant, the aunt had seen him. She had seen his stiff, distorted body; his shapeless, squashed and flattened head. The girl dug a hole in her diminutive graveyard. She laid him in his tomb with respect – with dignity, gravity, silence, respect – though the burial was barren of tears.

After the funeral, she tidied the graves and tended the flowers, then she left to sit on the gate. She sat alone till the early twilight, staring fixedly over the field, staring steadily out at the ley. Then, when darkness was truly dark, her aunt came out to her with some toast. They stayed together awhile in silence, looking out at the field.

It's getting cold.

—

The evenings are drawing in. The summer's blown. It's over.

—

I've spoken to your parents. The school term starts again next week. They're coming to pick you up.

—

They'll be here tomorrow night. Do you want to do anything special tomorrow? It'll be your last day.
No.
I've enjoyed having you here, you know. I've really enjoyed it. I hope it's been good for you, too.

—

The aunt's eyes sought out her niece. They sought for her face, and when they saw it, they found it blank of expression. Her whole body rigid and void of emotion. As if she was there but not there. The girl sat motionless on the gate. She was looking stolidly into the distance, looking beyond to the ley. Seeming oblivious of everything else. Night was creeping closer around them, folding them in and sinking upon them. The vestige of day was shrinking away; it was spilling its guts on the sea. A purple darkness had dripped from the sky, permeating the land. Light had been drained from the low horizon. Breath and form and shape were all gone.

The aunt shivered and returned to the farmhouse, leaving the girl to sit on the gate, to look out over the ley.

The Lure

It was her final evening. All day the girl had sat in her tree. She had been staring over the field to the ley; she had been watching the irksome reeds in their bed, tossing their heads in the wind. Occasionally, she had turned to the sea – smothered in sunlight, sunk in its sheen. She had glimpsed for a moment down to the yard, seeing the dogs in the drive. In the tree she was lost; removed from the world. She was hidden behind the quivering leaves, obscured by the shimmering light and the shade, swaying as one with the boughs.

Now it was dusk. The air was still. The valley was trapped beneath the weight of a purple cloud, which pressed close upon it, squeezing the light and the life from the land. The sea had receded; shackled and mute. The reeds shuffled misery from deep in the ley, resisting the forced tranquillity, awaiting the onset of storm.

The girl felt it, too. She felt the deceptive and unnatural stillness, the warmth and the moisture that hung on the air, the oppressive closeness, the anticipation of every creature around her. The cows stood close at the top of the field, in the shadow of the hunching hedge. The dogs lay uneasily, gnawing their paws, panting a weary restlessness in the loaded calm of the porch. A mouse was scurrying round the side of the barn.

She could see through a window into the kitchen; she could see the brightness that warmed from within burn off as it broke out into the yard; she could see her aunt – her torso, her hands – as she stood beside the busy sideboard, preparing the food for that evening.

She knew that soon they would be here.

She could picture the cat as it sat on the dresser, watching her aunt with its saucer eyes. She sensed Henry, standing alert in his stable, teasing the straw with impatient hooves. She sensed Rosie's vexations, lain in her sty, snorting an apprehensive grunt in the wretched solitude of the dark. She could hear the feet of rats in the barn; the bats as they tested their wings before flight; an owl as it shifted its perch on a beam.

Above the yard and the field beyond it, she saw a trace of abnormal light, superimposed on the bulging cloud. Then the lights themselves on the crest of the hill, adjusting and turning and falling away, defining the track which led to the farm, till a car came to rest in the drive. The lights and the engine were cut. The doors opened. Two people stepped out. Her parents.

Her aunt had heard them arrive. She was already opening the kitchen door, she was crossing the courtyard, she was greeting these people, she was shaking them both by the hand. Her father was taking a bag from the car, and now they were going inside – all three of them – into the kitchen, and into the warmth.

Through the window, the girl could see the shuffle of chairs as they sat. She could see the backs of the smiling dogs as they came to nuzzle their joy. She could see them all there, all flushed and expectant, as her aunt rose and pulled the blinds closed.

And now, there was only a muffled silence. For minutes, nothing at all. Then she heard the sudden click of a latch; she saw a shard of fickle light stirring the secretive yard.

Her aunt stepped into the gloom. She ambled over towards the tree. She raised her head and called up –

It's time.

The girl looked down on her aunt below, knowing she couldn't be seen within the solid clutch of the leaves. There could be no knowing, no way of knowing – not for certain – that the girl was there –

Come down.

But her aunt did know. She knew it was time. It was time. The girl uncurled herself from her branch. She shivered down through the drowning darkness, out and into the silver light. Together they went back into the house.

It was bright and warm inside. Her mother and father were sat at the table. They raised their heads as the girl came in.

She was wearing a white dress printed with flowers, smudged with grass stains and scrapings of earth. The hem was loose, the left sleeve was torn, and down the front there was blood. Over the dress was a cardigan, with holes at the elbow and snags at the waist. The girl wasn't wearing her shoes. Her head seemed huge for her fray of hair was clotted and clung with twigs and leaves. Her skin was scorched by the wind and the salt and the sun. It was scarred and lined, like an older woman's, though her face was unnaturally pale. Pale in the artificial light; pale and void of expression. She had a flat brow, a sloping nose, a pointed chin which was speckled with mud. She had pencil lips and vacant eyes – lips and eyes which said nothing. Her arms and her legs were muscular, lean. Her fingers and toes curled like claws.

Her parents rose and came to greet her. Her mother hugged her close. She knelt beside her, seeking her face, feeling her, kissing her hair. She hugged her more, and closer still, unwilling to loosen her hold. Then her father, too, bent down to her side, squeezing all three in a tight embrace. They led her back towards the table; they sat her between them where both could reach out. Reaching and touching and sharing their love.

She looked at these people, her parents. At their searching eyes, at their feeling hands, at the stupid joy which played on their mouths. She couldn't hear the words that they spoke; she seemed unable to give a reply. Instead, her aunt translated for her. She told of their early morning rounds, of the Judas tree, of her morning swims, of the ley, and the man who came to trap birds. And all of them listened in wonderment. They took in a fantasy so far removed from any world that they knew. They listened and took in her lies.

All through their meal, her parents watched her – they watched her, they reached out and touched her. Their restless fingers clasping her hands, stroking her skin, feeling into her coarse matted hair. Their distant faces smiling at her: smiling their fear and their love. They wanted to know from her all that was known; they wanted to take her straight home. They were stretching out further, they were straining to reach her, they were striving to close a divide. They wanted her, and the pain of that wanting sparkled as tears in their eyes.

After supper, the girl went outside to lock up, leaving the others alone. She rose, and closed the door on their pleas, muting and blunting their love.

Outside, the night was airless and still. She could feel the farm, and all within it, was caught in a cage of agitation, unsure and scarce daring to breathe. So too was the land. She crossed the yard towards the gate; she sat on the top bar facing the field, her eyes as ever upon the ley, feeling its never-ending being uncoiling somewhere below.

It was dark. Clouds closed out the hint of a moon, the trembling light of the stars. She could hear the suction of the sea sounding as a fainting echo, deep in the distance, beyond the dark, beyond the bounds of her sight. In front of her, only a stunning absence. Not sky nor land, nor the roll of a hill. Not even the field, which had drained away and was swallowed up in the pitch. In the immense, unfathomable blackness around her she sensed no forwards, no sideways, no backwards. She sensed no up and no down. There was only an infinite space and time, an eternity that stood for a fraction, that had no basis on which to exist save for the girl and the gate where she sat. No basis, save for this single moment. This moment she lived. This now. There was nothing else. No being nor meaning. There was nothing more. There was none.

Yet there was.

There was one other point she could see; one other source, one measure of being, fixed in the emptiness of the void. There, an immeasurable distance away, somewhere below her – perhaps in the field, perhaps in the reeds, perhaps on the farther side of the ley – there was light. A single point of brilliant light. Furious. And it was this, as much as the blanket of cloud, as much as the overbearing night, that had turned her world into pitch.

A light that shot heat through the frozen blackness. A blinding light from a single beam. She brought her hands towards her face, screening her eyes from the pain of seeing, as she gauged what and where it might be. It didn't waver. It didn't move. It rose, imperious, staring upwards, all-powerful, scarring the sky. Magical, grotesque, huge. It was burning white; it was bitterly cold. It was piercing the night with its searing heat. It was calling to her, demanding she came.

From somewhere behind her, she heard her aunt's voice. It was time for her to go in. The dogs were waiting for her on the porch, eager to retreat to the warmth. The girl took one last long look at the light, then she slipped off the gate and ran inside.

Inside, her parents stood in the kitchen, watching and waiting for her. They had wanted to go outside with her; they wanted to be with her still. They wanted her back. They wanted her with them so much right now they might have crushed her ribs in their arms; they might have lured her into the car and driven her over the hill. They might have torn her from the farm. They had seen her aunt; they had seen the love and the trust in her face; they had seen what lay beyond reach. They could see the bond between the two in the way they moved around the room, in the print of their footsteps, their single breath. They could feel its power, its strength of connection. Irresistible and merciless. More than they could endure.

So, they did the only thing they knew. They drew her to them; they stroked her skin. They saw her safely into her room – safe for the night, and safe in their love. They kissed her and turned off her light.

The girl heard the door close behind her. She got off her bed and went to the window, pressing her face up close to the pane, staring into beyond. Beyond, she couldn't see the light, yet she knew it still there by the spectral glare that washed over the field as a silver wave. She returned to her bed and lay fully clothed, counting out sound round the house.

There was a bathroom above her. To one side was her aunt's room, whilst on the other was a large spare room with a bed. She listened and waited. She could hear the creak of the kitchen door; the yawn of dogs as they settled for sleep. From above, she could hear the running of water; the clink and the wheeze of a metal bin; then the dual motion – a clunk and a click – of a pull-string light being tugged. She counted out time in her mind. Three minutes, four minutes, five. She heard the tread of bed-bound feet, then the desperate hush of a stunning silence. Deliberately, she counted out five minutes more, each second tolled in slow time.

And now, from the rasping, deadened silence, she knew there was no more disturbance.

The girl sat up and inspected her window. It was high and small, and hinged at the top, with a handle-lock at its base. She brought up a chair beneath the window, then turned the handle and pushed. The base of the frame extended outward into the evening air. She judged there was just enough space. She thrust her head through the gap and looked down. The drop to the ground was five feet. She pulled her head back from the opening. She put on her coat and her grey woollen cap. Then she listened out again through the silence, ensuring all were asleep.

She counted out another slow minute – one lucky minute – there in the absolute calm. Then she climbed on the chair and thrust her legs – one after the other – out of the window. She balanced her body on top of the frame, rolling her stomach and tucking her head, inching and squirming herself through the gap, till she clung to the frame by only her arms, with her feet hanging free on the wall. She straightened her arms to ease herself down, then let go and fell onto the grass.

The girl looked round. There was the stunning point of light, hung in the shapeless depth of the dark. Still there, and still just as bright. She was drawn to it, seductively drawn. First, though, she went to the tool shed. She took a short ladder and stood it beneath the window which led to her room. Then she looked again towards the house, searching its face and searching its eyes for a lamp, for motion, for life. Only when certain that all were asleep, she slipped like a shadow down through the field, inexorably drawn to the light.

The girl crouched low, creeping down the arch of the field. She could see the light directly now, wrapped round within a fainting glow, and hung in all-pervasive night. And yet she couldn't place its source, nor judge its distance from herself. She stole towards it furtively – intrigued, enthralled, unsure. Feeling it drawing her into its power; feeling it mesmerise her. She thought it would have served to guide her, but it didn't show her the way. It was too proud, too noble, too strong. The light she saw was the only light, and everything beyond that light was sightlessness, was a void. A vacuum; a nothingness. An empty stage on which she trod, on which she felt her feeling footsteps fade and fall away.

She sneaked by instinct through the grass, along the paths of dusk and dawn which every day she carved by day, which now she conjured in her mind. She felt her steps steal down the slope, sinking further into darkness, closing on the field's fringe.

Now, suddenly, the barbed wire fence reared up ahead of her. She changed direction, striking out in parallel, counting out the posts. She strained her eyes in front of her, resisting the allure, the urge to make straight for the light.

The first earth-hedge rose tall before her, looming, massive, in her path, making her recoil in shock although she knew it there. She stared at its immobile bulk, its huge and hostile heap of hate, seeking for the passageway between the fence and hedge. And there, two feet away from her, the solid blackness fell away, the second field emerged.

She paused again to face the light. It burned more brightly still. More brilliant than when she first had seen it, when sitting on the gate. She saw it bigger, closer now, though still she didn't know how close. Its source might be within the reeds, or on the far side bank, or even in the field beyond. It might be in the sky. It burned pure, frigid white. Enticing, frightening, all-beguiling. Stabbing at her unclosed eyes, throbbing in her brain.

She switched her gaze back to the ground, wanting to absorb the dark, wanting to adapt to gloom. To calm and accustom her eyes. The earth was a pool of empty blackness. She could see her feet, but not the ground — neither before nor beneath her. Somewhere near, she knew there would be a scraping under the wire.

She dropped to her knees, feeling the rub of the fence on her shoulder, feeling it firm in her hand. From here she could almost see the grass, and the lie of the field around her. She crawled on all fours, forwards slowly, her eyes fixed on the foot of the fence, her left hand trawling the clumpy grass beneath the bottom-most wires. She closed her eyes deliberately, allowing her fingers to guide her.

Ten feet. Fifteen. Twenty.

Her palms were scratched by the brambles and thistles which grew unchecked by the fence. The joints of her fingers were cut and raw from clawing close to the wire. Then her left hand felt a divot of earth. She stopped and peered – her face no more than a foot from the ground.

Here, below her – right before her – the turf was crisp and grey. The grass was dead. She plucked at a lump and felt it yield. This was the trench she had dug. As she had before, all summer long, she slithered under the fence, pulling the divots behind her. Now she was here, she was where she belonged, in the sanctuary of the ley.

She sat with her back to the fence, raising her eyes to the light once more. It was immeasurable, and immense. So scintillating, so fascinating, she felt compelled to approach. She felt an urge to dive through the reeds, to touch it, to burn within it, to drown. Unable to resist that desire, she got to her feet, she slid down the bank, she struck out straight for the ley. Then something checked her. A single image, fierce and focused, projected deep in her mind. She pictured the reeds – looking down through the reeds – looking down at the brackish still water. And there upon it, there within it, there was her own distorted face staring at her with sightless eyes.

The girl sat tight against the fence, feeling the welcome press of the wire cutting into her skin. Feeling secure for feeling its hurt. Once more, she stared out over the ley, seeing a single tassel of reed silhouetted against the sheer light. She bent forwards slowly, lowering her head. Now she could see there were many tassels, all brushing the path of the beam. She lay on her side, and the light was eclipsed behind the body of reed. Then the light couldn't be in the opposite field. It must be just there on the bank.

To see it she knew she would need to be closer. She knew to be closer she must go through the ley. To go through the ley when she could not see, she knew to mean she would drown. She must surely drown.

She felt the lattice of wire in her fingers; she felt the firm of the earth where she sat. She wrapped herself in its cruel reason, knowing she had to go back.

She paused. Without even needing to look towards it, the girl was aware of the light. More than aware. Enraptured. She could sense the purity of its whiteness suspended in a stunning black void. She could sense its sheer intensity scouring her sanity. She knew in her heart she couldn't go back. Even when here, when clung to the fence, she knew she couldn't resist. She had to touch it. She had to know it. She convinced herself that sight wasn't needed to find her path through the ley. She was part of its body, part of its being. She and the ley were as one. She would be able to feel her way through, guided by instinct alone.

From the scraping behind her, and from where she had crawled, she knew where to enter the reeds. She slipped to the track and crawled along it, pacing the distance by counting the steps she took on her hands and her knees.

Here, in the darkness beside the mudbed, she moved with more confidence than when in the field. She knew this track like she knew her skin; she could trace every pore in her mind. Each furrow, each wrinkle, each dip, each crevice, was known to her feet and her hands.

She moved rhythmically, easily, down the blind track. When she knew she was close to the path through the ley she relaxed and rolled down the bank. She rolled till she tasted the sweat of the ley – its stale moist tang on her tongue. She opened her eyes, and here before her were the long, thin limbs of the reeds. She spread her fingers and felt through the scrub, inch by inch, her hands palm-downwards, seeking her bearing by touch. Then she felt something certain – a scatter of stones – the pebbles she used to mark the path that very first time she had come.

The girl stood up beside the reeds. They rose above her, tall and close-ranked. Only their tassels and uppermost leaves whispered a warning to her. Enter and drown. Enter and die. Die a long and listless death. Never more to be seen. Enter, and be one with the ley. Come, and become what we are. Come and become one of us. They shivered against the empty air, against the stillness of the still night. They stood abreast, impenetrable, rank after measureless rank in their millions, with a spectral sliver of pure white light catching the crests of their heads.

The girl closed her eyes. She opened her mind. She opened her mind to the ley. She thought herself into being within it. She thought herself woven into its fabric. An indelible part – merely one of their millions – the same as them. Just the same. She waited until she came into focus, till she felt herself becoming as them, till she knew herself as a single reed in the clattering, chattering throng. All around her, her brothers and sisters. Their sound her sound, her movement as theirs: sighing and soothing and shuffling as one. As one, she entered their brittle fold, feeling their hollow stems striking her shoulders, feeling them clutch at her feet. She stuttered their scorn; she shivered their torment; she swayed with her brethren, backwards and forwards, and forwards and onwards and through. She and they were a single being, a single motion, a single sound. Integral and absolute.

She sensed their shared body tighten and tense as she slipped deeper into its core. Their clamour as one huge scream of anguish, chanted and piercing the night. Their groaning and panting fierce on her ear; their limbs a tortured caress. Their leaves as knives which sliced at the dark, thrashing and shearing their tendons. Their single mass collapsing and writhing, stinging itself with its hate. And she as they, at the heart of it all, sunk in the bedlam, drunk on their agony, grinning their wretched despair.

From somewhere inside them, from inside herself, she felt their madness melting to reason, their panic placated, their senses restored. She reached out her arms to those that were round her, feeling about her their own feeling hands. They were fading and stilling; now standing in silence; now gradually petering out. Their vast song was being draw from their lips, their secrets spent and now gone. She felt her body no longer their body. She felt herself on her own. Only then, when entirely stripped of her kin, did the girl dare open her eyes.

She was standing on a bald patch of grass. She had reached the bank on the farther side.

She looked up. There, fifty yards up ahead, near the hut, she could see the light, untarnished, in full. She could see it radiate from the bank – a sheer, supreme, and perfect light. Absolute light in absolute darkness. An infinite radiance; an irrepressible glory. Complete in itself. Entire.

She felt powerless before it, compelled to touch it. She found she was moving swiftly forwards, her arms outstretched, her lips apart as if she were able to breathe it in. It seemed to her the essence of light, the source of all light, the giver of light. As strong as the sun, as serene as the moon. It was space and time collapsed into one.

Then she stopped. She dropped to her knees, flat on her stomach, her head pressed hard in the grass. For precious seconds she lay unmoving, unsure of what she had seen. Then, gradually, she raised herself; she looked again at the light. There was no mistaking it now.

There, before her, locked in the light, was an outlined torso and head. There was a person, low and still in the grass, sitting in front of the beam. They were staring into its soul. The girl lay quite still while she watched them. Then she eased herself forwards at the base of the bank, where the roll of the slope and the darkness hid her, with scarcely a motion or sound.

Now she was only ten feet away. She peered from the fringe of the bank. The person was kneeling down by the light, their fingers weaving in and around it, seeming to revel within its sheer splendour. Their body was bent in mute surrender, as if they were captured in prayer. Above the steady silence of beauty, she could hear a mechanical throbbing nearby.

The girl turned back towards the light. She could see it clearly – both the beam and its source. It was raised on what seemed like a wide-mouthed bucket, with a white neck collar, and a sheet of glass laid above like a shelf. It was pure, so pure. It shone like a truth. Though the face of that truth was sullied, impure – a scatter of haphazard dots fluttered round it, breaking the cast of its perfect beam, spoiling and blemishing its sheen.

The girl crept still closer, wanting to see who the person was and what they were doing. Needing to witness the light. The person sat with their back towards her, so all she could see was their outlined frame against the wash of the light. They sat unmoving, save for their hands; their frame appeared slender and frail. She watched at their fingers stroking the light, their body quite still, in silent homage, seeming enthralled by the beam.

Then, through the wonder of their devotion, over the sound of the engine nearby, she saw the person raising their arms as they bent to examine the light. For the first time, she saw their arms clearly. She saw the right arm lift up the glass; she saw the left arm follow behind. It was awkward, unsure, like a broken wing. In that moment, she knew who it was. She knew them as well as she knew the ley. It wasn't a random person before her. It was him.

She recognised his movement at once. And, as she did so, instinctively, she was edging backwards, she was crawling away. A sudden panic rose as a rash, confusing her senses, her mind. It was only now that she was aware of where she was and how she had got here, and who was waiting for her. In that instant, the knowledge came to her clearly, deriding her folly, mocking her innocence.

She was here, in the ley, on its farther side. She couldn't retreat; she couldn't escape. She could picture no way of returning. She was trapped on her own; she was here in the darkness. She was trapped in the darkness. Alone.

The man turned round and got up from his knees. He stood. He started coming towards her. He had seen her. He started to speak.

The girl arose in a single motion, ready to throw herself at the reeds, to bury herself in their blinded body, to blur in their depths and be gone. But they wouldn't let her, they wouldn't yield. She wasn't a part of the ley anymore. She had left it; she couldn't return. She was fixed to the bank; she was rooted to that. All she could do was to stare at the man: to watch him come forward, to watch him approach. To watch as his body rose before her and steadily blacked out the light.

He had reached her now. Just one pace away. Even less than one pace. He was looking straight at her – looking into her face. Then he smiled and held out his hand. He grasped onto hers. He led her up the bank to the light. The girl knew she was powerless, that she could do nothing. There was nowhere to go, and nothing but darkness. He took her towards the incredible brightness; he knelt her down to its side. Till it filled her vision and was all that she saw. Till it stole and stared into her heart.

The core of the light was pure white. An absolute white. It was brilliant, without being blinding. It stood above the jaws of a bucket four feet wide and three feet deep, with egg cartons lining the floor. And crawling over the cardboard cartons – beneath them, around them, through them, within them – was a teeming army of moths.

She raised her eyes to the shaft of light which rose and tore at the sky, and through it she saw their shadowed world was frantic with fluttering moths. On her jacket and trousers, on the ground around her, on the person who knelt to her side. Clouds of moths were crowding the light, creeping down the white-necked funnel, sliding into the bucket beneath, or stood upside down on the glass. They were basking, opening and closing their wings. They were worshipping the sheer light.

The girl felt her wrist being squeezed. She turned. The man's hand was laid on her arm. She stared at him, frozen, unable to move –

Put out your hand and hold it still.

The girl obeyed. The man placed a sugar lump into her palm. He spat on the cube, then used his finger to crush it and stir it into a paste. He licked his finger clean with his tongue.

He told the girl to come closer to him, to stretch out her palm and lay it flat, to hold her body quite still. Again, the girl did as she was told. She could feel the invisible world about her, fanned by the silence of quivering flight. She could see the night sky fierce with life, fractured and torn by a feverish patchwork, by the pulse of thousands of wings. And from that sky, moths came to her hand. She could feel their weightlessness in her palm. Their stout, hairy bodies; their silken faces; their broken delicate legs.

The girl looked up. The air was choked and alive with moths. In the light; in the darkness; beyond the dark. Beyond the reach of all sight. They came to feast, and still they came – as though the sky was knitted of moths, comprised of nothing but wings. The man beside her muttered their names as each one came to land in her hand. The girl was enticed by the magical sounds –

How long will the moths keep coming?
They could come all night. Until dawn.
How long will you stay here?
All night.
Won't you get tired?
There's a room at the back of the hut if you want to bed down.

They sat silently watching the moths. Their fragile sphere came closer still. All about them a blanket of blackness – ponderous and warm – encircled their wonderful light. The air was motionless, breathless. The sky a flutter of life. There was no sense of any existence beyond. This spectral universe was all. The girl grew drowsy in its thrall; her body curled as she knelt. The man beside her witnessed these things. He put out his hand to the girl –

Come.

He led the girl away from the light, his footsteps soundless and true. Together they climbed the slope of the bank. Together they entered the hut.

The girl felt a dampness pinching her face. A raw, an uncomfortable wetness. She turned in her sleep, as if wanting to hide her head in her pillow, seeking the warmth of her sheet. But her face couldn't be hidden.

Again, she felt the sting of the wetness. And, with it, a harsh and unwelcoming light. Bright on her tight-closed eyelids. She wanted only to sleep. She felt so tired, and her body ached. She hugged her limbs, but could find no warmth, no retreat from the light that wouldn't relent.

Reluctantly, she opened her eyes.

It was early morning, shapeless and soundless. Above her a blanket of thick folds of cloud hung low and grey in the sky. The land was all washed out. The colour drained from its skin. Even the grass was colourless. She could feel the drizzle dampening her face.

She turned. It was painful turning, painful to move. Her cheek was laid in a patch of mud. Beyond the mud was a gate. Her gate. The gate that led to the farm. She turned again, raising her head from the mud. Yes, it was as she thought. She was here – she was on the cold hill's side, in the field, at the top of her field. In front of her was a wash of grass which stretched away down the slope. Beyond it the ley, lined silver-grey. And over the dune was the dull slate sea. The clouds were pregnant with rain.

She tried to rise, but her legs resisted. She was cold; her body was sodden through. She could feel the sleek wind cutting the air, bringing yet denser wreathes of cloud. She was all alone in the field. There was nothing around her. Nothing here. No people, no cows, no crows. No sight nor sound of any birds. And no song.

She dragged herself to the side of the house, pulling at clumps of grass with her hands. She reached the wall beside her bedroom; her window was open above her.

The steps were still where she placed them last night, but she knew herself unable to climb. She pulled her body up to a sit, then slumped against the brick wall. She hugged her knees up into her chest, shivering warmth through her limbs.

Then came the rain. It came on full. She winced as she felt it prickling her cheeks, biting her body, stinging her skin. It cut from the cloud and pierced the earth, fierce against the face of the house, bouncing off the tiled roof. The ley blurred into a green-grey shape; it was lost in a solid, silver-white curtain slicing into the ground. The sea was soaked up into the cloud. The field creased its agony. The noise. The girl hid within the slight shield of her knees, protecting her face with tortured arms. The wind was snatching and pinching at her. It slapped at her body and howled. She felt herself bullied by squall after squall; by shrieking rain exploding about her, screaming into the earth.

Then, there was a lessening. The rain, the wind, the noise all slackened. Their fury faltered and fell away. In the pre-dawn grey, the girl looked up. The day was washed out and wan. Void of colour, expression and form. Now there was only the rain. The simple rain. It was falling but faintly; it was falling slow. It was washing and cleansing the brutalised earth. It was washing away the sins of the world.

The girl looked down towards the ley. There, amongst the withering sedge, she could see the man as he stumbled onwards, as he disappeared into the reedbed.

The Shedding

The aunt was first to the kitchen that morning. Since she knew it to be the girl's last day, she thought they might walk round the yard together, sharing the animals one last time – patting them, feeding them, talking soft words – as the girl took her leave of them all. But the girl wasn't where she expected to see her, awaiting her aunt in the kitchen. And, when footsteps finally came, they were slow, with the weighted tread of an adult. Her parents had also awoken early. It was they who were eager to walk round the farm – as if that knowledge would help to explain why their daughter had spent all this time with her aunt, as if to explain what she had become.

The parents strolled out to the beckoning yard. There, to the side of the older woman; there, in the space that was left by the girl. They followed, they watched, they asked constant questions; they wanted to know her routine. When they were done, they returned to the kitchen, flushed with the clear morning air. Breakfast came, and breakfast was eaten; but there was still no sign of the girl. Her parents assumed she had gone down the field to witness the ley for a final time. They respected her freedom, they waited for her, secure in the knowledge that now she was theirs – that soon they would take her back home.

It was ten o'clock. The adults sat alone in the kitchen, waiting for the girl to return. The parents were urgent to see their daughter; they wanted to set off and start off anew. The aunt was aware that the girl was still here, and wrapped herself round in the warmth of that knowledge.

They talked their pretence in sentences with no beginning and no fixed end: their eyes and ears to the door. At last, the mother could bear it no more. She said she would go and finish the packing in readiness for the girl. She rose and went from the room. The father and aunt were left in the kitchen, in a space with no meaning, no words.

Then, through the infinite distance of silence, they heard a cry from within.

Both he and she went into the hall. The mother was stood in her daughter's doorway. Rooted and fixed; not looking at them. She seemed unsteady, as if ready to fall. They came to her and took hold of her arms. They followed her gaze through the room.

There was the bed, made up and not slept in. There were the bags, all packed with her clothes. There was a sliver of tender sunlight. And there, within it, the girl.

She was straddling the base of a narrow window, with a leg either side of the glass. Her body was lying prone on the frame, her head tucked into a ball on her chest, her wide eyes staring, not seeing. Not seeming to breathe.

Her father pushed between the two women, pulling the girl from the open window, laying her down on the bed. She was sodden and stiff. She was cold to the touch. Her dress and her face were covered in mud. Her clothes were drenched. Her feet were cold-blue and bare.

Her aunt reached out to feel for a pulse. It was there.

The women removed her clothes. There were scratches and bruises around her neck, and more on her shoulders and arms. Her aunt came back with a bowl of warm water, and between them they washed the girl down.

The girl lay silent and still. She didn't shiver; she didn't move. Not even her fingers, her eyes. She didn't seem to know they were there; she didn't seem to know who they were. They laid her out on her bed. They put a layer of blankets around her, and hot bottles flanking her limbs. Both mother and aunt attended the girl; both bustling and busy beside her. When all they could think of to do had been done, the women drew the curtains tight closed and stood alone in the gloom. For precious minutes they stood apart, unwilling to go from the room.

The aunt returned to the hollow kitchen. She measured coffee into a jug; she stared into the vacant yard as the kettle came to a boil. She brought the cups to the kitchen table, and there both she and the father sat, facing each other in silence. There was nothing to say. Nothing to do. Nothing that either could comprehend. The coffee cooled in their cups, untouched. Beyond the window, the morning grew, it grew in brilliance, in pure striking radiance. It burned away the stain of grey which had settled over the dawn. It revealed a beautiful day.

In the room next door, the mother sat by her daughter. Watching her, watching her. Her long thin body lay quite still, her legs together, her arms to her sides, her eyes unmoved from the wall. A gradual warmth was entering her frame, but her skin stayed pallid and dull. Her mother attempted talking to her, but her words were noise without meaning. There was no recognition; not a move of the head nor a spark in the eye; the body seemed drained and sucked dry. The mother continued to stare at her daughter, as if a stare could breathe her to life. This child that she knew to still be alive – so vital, so urgent, so charged full of life. She brought her chair to the bed.

She snatched the girl's hand selfishly – pressing it, wanting to feel the pressure returned. She was close to her daughter now. So close. So very close, so near. Just she and her daughter, here together. Right here, where she had never been. Where she had always wanted to be.

Lunchtime came. The girl lay still, neither sleeping nor waking. Her aunt watched over her from a chair. Her parents stood apart in the kitchen, attempting to reason with fear. They wanted their daughter, they wanted her back – back in London, with them. Here, on the farm, she was not their daughter: she was someone that neither he nor she knew. Here, before them, in front of them, they could see her dissolving away. They were losing her with each moment that passed; they were losing her even while watching. Here they knew she could not be helped, here she could not be cured. The farm was the symptom and cause of her pain. Their love – that unspent energy – told them they needed to take her back home. They knew they had to take her away. The hurt they might cause by moving her would surely be less than the promise of healing once they were safely in London.

Stung by the strength, the resolve of their love, they went together into her room. Between them they eased the girl from her bed, they shuffled the body towards the door. The father took hold of the girl's stiffened shoulders; her mother clutched onto her legs. The girl was paralysed, heavy, inert. She didn't resist; she was still. They knocked past the aunt and into the hall; then through the front door they came. When they entered the courtyard, the pitiless sun spat its gloss in her face.

The girl screamed.

It was a huge scream for someone so small. A high, endless note, without pitch or form. Sprung from deep in her chest. It chased along the length of her spine and shuddered her frame with its strength. It was neither an angry, nor fearful cry. It was untamed, unbounded, wild.

The parents sought each other's eyes – their love, their purpose destroyed. Without speaking, they went back to the house, they placed the girl on her bed. Behind them, they could hear her scream lingering in the concrete yard. They could hear it dying a death on the air as the wind dispersed it round the farm, as it melted away in the sun.

All day the mother and aunt took turns to sit by the side of the girl. The girl didn't move, nor utter a word. She lay on her back; she stared at the ceiling with vacant unblinking eyes. She wouldn't eat, but they helped her up and spilt water into her mouth. She didn't seem able to sleep, nor to want to. Her body was neither hot nor cold. There was no sign of fever, no clear distress. The women wrapped her close in the blankets, cooling her brow with dampened towels, urging the body to life.

Supper. The adults sat alone in the kitchen. Silence more comfort than speech. They had tried to talk, they had wanted to talk – fearing their own and the others' fears – but conversation became speculation, and speculation despair. They knew only nothing. The nothing she told them. They imagined it all, and none of it kind. Each, in their own minds, different, the same. Sat round the table, sharing one meal, perfectly crippled, each quite alone. The girl, their daughter, was close to them here. So close, so protected, so loved. Yet nothing they did nor tried to do could touch her, could reach her, could heal her.

Their love was uttered in unheard whispers; their love was projected through unfelt hands. And they knew the frailty of that love by its failure to touch or take hold of the girl. Their meal ended, they broke apart, each to their own paralysis. All night they vied to take turns in her room, to watch the girl as she lay.

The next morning the women worked together, lifting the girl up and into the bath. They supported her, with arms outstretched; they washed her, they dressed her, they brushed her hair. Then between them they carried her back to her room; they sat her up in the bed and fed her. They urged her body to life.

The girl's arms and legs were senseless and useless, her eyes without knowing, her face blank. She seemed to breathe without sound. She didn't speak, nor appear to hear. They knew her alive, but she wasn't living. She didn't seem to want to live. Or to know how to live. Or why. The two women sat on the bed beside her, watching her as she lay. The pain of being with her was as nothing compared to the pain of being without. When not in her room, they sat in the kitchen feigning to read or to sleep. They looked out onto the brilliant day – so clear and fine and full of life – and shielded its warmth from their eyes.

Another day. Then another. Each the same – the same empty day, filled with false promise and pain. On the fourth, her father departed for London. Not wanting to go, unable to stay. Here, with this. Where silence shrieked in his wanting ears, where minutes failed to move on.

In his absence, the women tended the girl, dividing the days between watching and resting; together rarely, and always apart. Both channelling the strength and the sum of their love at the thin white body laid out on the bed in the room in the heart of the farm. Both wished only to be with the girl, selfish for wanting to give. The girl was their comfort, their grief, their despair. Through the windows, the blind sun rose every day; it arched through the sky and set on the sea, bleeding its dying rays on the waves. The dogs sat unwalked and unloved on the porch; the cows grazed unmilked in the empty field; Henry stared at the barren yard, waiting for someone to come.

After a week, they noticed a change. A flicker of life in her eyes. A sense of seeing, a sense of being, for elusive fractions of time. They saw that her eyes would seem to glide from object to object around the room. But then they would stop, they would lock onto blankness, glazing and gliding to vacancy. Then there was nothing alert about her; nothing to show she could see. Then, if by chance her eyes should meet theirs, they could see there was no recognition. There was nothing to show of the child that once was but the random drift of those eyes.

What happened?

—

What's wrong?

—

Where are you hurt?

—

I love you. Come back to me. Please.

More days passed. The mother and aunt brought flowers to the room. They brought a branch from the Judas tree. They told the girl stories; they sang her songs; they held her; they searched for a token of life.

The room where she lay was close and airless; it smelt of emptiness and disuse. All that entered decayed. The flowers died. The leaves withered. The songs were swallowed by deadened silence, and their hope was blunted by dust. Words had no meaning; no beginning, no end; they drifted into the ether. Helpless, both women struggled for life; they opened the windows to breathe.

The girl appeared to smell the air as it secretly stole through the room. She turned her head to the window briefly, then rolled away as though in pain, shrinking into herself. Her mother came up close to the girl, placing her hands on her face. She could feel the broken body tighten, the muscles tense as she lay.

The next morning, they determined to move her. They took her upstairs to a corner room which looked out on three sides of the farm. From here the shifting day took form – from the courtyard at dawn, to the field at noon, to the sunken sea at twilight. The sun tinged the walls with a softened pink, that grew to a blush of brilliant gold, that melted to cream, that thickened to crimson, that coarsened to grey, that closed in around her – bloodied and cruel – as the last strands of daylight faded away. All through the day they sat beside her, watching and waiting and hoping and listening. Catching each word that was never spoken; returning each look that was never made. The girl's eyes wandered around the room. Her latticed fingers lay in her lap. Her hair was brushed and caught in a ribbon. Her lips were thin and so pale.

That day, and in the days that came next, they lifted the girl from the bed where she lay and sat her down in a chair. From here she could look out through the window.

She could look beyond and into the yard. From here she might see a dog on the porch; or her aunt with a bucket of feed; or Henry looking out from his stall; or simply the spill of the wanton sun. When not in the room, her mother would stand in the yard beneath where she sat. She would look up and smile, and sometimes she waved. She would see the silent shape of the girl through slivers of shivering glass. And, as she looked, as she searched with her eyes, she prayed that her look was returned.

Each day, they brought up meals for the girl. They fed her, they put the food in her hand and brought that hand to her mouth. They moved her chair to follow the sun. They moved her body from chair to bed. They gave her water, propped up on her pillows. They read, they talked, they listened to silence. They sat through the night with a small light burning. At times they even faltered to sleep.

The girl did not sleep. But she wasn't awake. She saw nothing; heard nothing; felt nothing within. Somewhere, perhaps, there might have been feeling. But if so, she didn't own what that was. She couldn't feel the feelings inside her, or know where they came from, or why they should come. She couldn't feel pain, though she felt that she had – that her body had known pain before. Only, perhaps, in the heart of the night, in the secret hush of a sleeping house, then perhaps she could see. The long beams that stretched high over her head, leading off to a secretive world. The bricks in the fireplace opposite, laid almost exactly but not quite square. The arching back of a rocking chair, the shape of a wave suspended in time. A long black tube which sparkled with jewels, piping sounds to a distant shore where a strange girl stood by the fringe of the sea, writing her name in the sand.

Her mother and aunt taught the girl how to walk; how to wash and dress; how to eat. She was slow to learn, and not keen on learning. She resisted the knowledge they brought. Each day, she rose with the dawn, watching the sun as it stole from its bed, watching it colour the waiting world, watching the yard creep to life. She learned how to stand, how to sit in her chair. She learned how to open one of the windows so she could let in the air. She learned the sound of a barking dog, the scrape of a horse's hoof in the yard, the distant cry of a bird.

Colour returned to her skin. Her flesh grew warm. She learned how to smile – a gradual smile that seemed to stop on the cusp of sense. Her eyes grew steady and glazed into focus. They thought she might speak had she tried. When they entered her room, she raised her head as if she acknowledged them there. Touching her hand, they sometimes found she would look at them, she would seem to know them. When thirsty she drank. When hungry she ate. She did this herself, and secretly. Always alone, and never when watched. When either woman came into her room, she was there, sitting quiet and still.

Her aunt thought the presence of animals might help the girl with her healing. She thought they might spark a remembrance in her, or might kindle a flicker of feeling. She thought that their innocence, the touch of their fur, might bring the girl back to life. The aunt encouraged a dog up the stairs; she brought it as far as the door. But when the girl saw it coming towards her – furiously panting its joy and its love – she curled in her chair and shrank from the creature. Instead, the aunt thought she might go to the ley, she might ask the man to bring up a bird, so the girl could see it and could let it go free.

Day followed night. The girl grew accustomed to objects and actions, if their purpose still appeared vague. The courtyard, and all the being within it, gradually entered her known. Each animal. Its sound and its habit. Each subtle shade of the day. Then there came a day when her mother found the girl looking out on the ley. She found her looking with distant eyes on a broader world, a richer world. As though she had tired of the yard.

From then on, it was always the ley. Always and only the ley. Her singular focus, her sole point of interest. The sea, the land, the sky, the ley. The girl looked tirelessly from her window, absorbed in all that she saw. Mother and aunt were encouraged, afraid. They could see her connecting with what lay beyond – through the window and down through the field. It was stirring with life, and its life-giving force was instilling life into the girl.

So they gave her the space to nurture herself. Now they stopped holding vigil each night. When they entered at dawn, she was already seated, she was staring out at the ley. When they looked up at her from the yard by day, her outline was gone, there was only a shadow. Now she was looking away. All day the girl would sit by the window, as the colours shifted, the clouds rolled through, the winds picked up and died. As they wished her goodnight she would turn and smile – just for an instant, and just for so long – before switching back to the ley.

Then, one day, whilst arranging some flowers, the aunt heard the sound of a voice. The long-forgotten sound of a voice, of the voice of a child, in the room –

I'm ready to go home now.

She started and turned – frightened, delighted by what she had heard. The girl was sitting beside the window, staring out to that other world. Staring intently, caught in the moment, as if those words had never been spoken. But so true the words, and so real.

That was all she would say. There were no more words. In the time it took for her mother to pack, for her father to drive to the farm to collect them, the girl continued to look out afar – out to the reeds and the sea. So distant, it almost felt to the women that the girl was no longer here. She was no longer in or a part of the room. She was there. She was elsewhere. She was somewhere out there. Somewhere far beyond reach. Both the women felt it and knew it. They knew she had gone, she had slithered away, right from under their care. She had gone so far, and so secretly, they feared she wouldn't return. The mother, at least, had the comfort of presence, for she knew she would still see her child. But for the aunt, there was no such compassion. She had nothing more than a memory. A memory that was already dying, that was dying before it was born. She would have clasped the girl to her breast; she would have clung to her, bleeding her dry. But nothing could come of that but sorrow. So she saved her tears for herself. For when she could hide herself in her room; for when there was no one to see. For when she could wrap herself in her grief, and face the fear that she owned. When loneliness could break on its own. When woe could surface with all of its pain, in all its immensity.

That evening, a car drove into the yard. The girl came out and was hugged by her aunt as if for a final time. She got in the car, and was driven away, turning her back on the ley.

The Revenge

Earth. The body of land a curvaceous shape of hills and valleys and fields; of hunchbacked trees, of clumps of bush, of hedges hewn from the soil. Water. A giddy mass, forming itself into infinite beings for elusive fractions of time; melting into the liquid ether as it stretches out beyond sight. Wind and fire. The ley, couched in the valley of the body of earth, its head in the lap of its mother, the sea. A shock of sudden pools and potholes; of natural traps and snares. Thrashed by the wind, burned by the sun, mocked by the chattering reeds. Not earth nor water. Somewhere between. A borderland, a micro world, bringing to life and taking away. Living and growing, surviving and dying – caught in a cycle of constant renewal – consuming and feeding its own.

Summer bore autumn, bore winter. The sea spewed its salt in the mouth of the ley, forcing it open to drink of it deep, till the sullen waters were stirred into life. Leaden skies emptied their spiteful load as they met with the desolate land. Rain polished the fields and spun down their sides, chasing their contours and flooding the valley, choking and drowning the reeds. Channels of brackish water appeared, furrowing the face of the ley. A furious wind scratched its feverish surface. The reeds bent in agony, creased by the slaughter, screaming a foul-mouthed wretchedness, weighted down by the pain. Nights came early, hungry and long; howling a misery that chilled to the soul. At times, uneasy stillness fell; a coolness, a freshness, an emptiness; an absence having no end. Then, in the greyness of flaccid unbeing, the world was undone. The ley lost its shape and fell into silence.

Mornings were breathless and sharp. The day's nervous fingers clawed at the land, shivering a light which never quite warmed, which never quite brought into life.

Colours shifted, clouds rolled through, winds picked up and died. Then a crack in the cloud. The faintest of rays from a searching sun caressing the fabric of earth. Somewhere, a snowdrop. Bluebells, a primrose. A noise in the fields of nature returning. A robin perched low in the Judas tree. Damp early mornings, bright and alert. A shimmering sea that shivered with motion, sucking its breath through its teeth. The reedbed thickened, ecstatically green. The sun scorched its tips and bronzed its curtains, setting the valley on fire. The ley grew pregnant with the promise of life, sweating and sighing a warm embrace between the thighs of the field. Birds re-entered the crowded haven, seeking retreat and safe harbour. Seeking love on the wing. Nests were made amidst the haste of furious feeding, feuding, existing. The ley was vibrant, pulsing with being, filled with the urgent chorus of life.

The farm stood alone to face the seasons, exposed on the slope of the field. Rain carved into its hard stone walls; wind sliced into its skin. The sun baked its sinews, crumbling its mortar, poking rude fingers into a body that once had been noble and strong.

Imperceptibly, year after year, the farm was eroded and ruptured. Its stones were loosened, its tiles tugged free, the earth on which it stood was reshaped. The building tired beneath its own weight, accepting its gradual decay. The stable doors were opened and closed. Animals entered and left. The hopeful and innocent cries of birth, the certain and echoing groans death, spilling their music into the yard, aging it through the passage of time, till the space was captured by silence. Dogs stayed faithful and proud, ears flapping like flags as they stood their guard, as they greeted and loved, till the end. A person marched, bent-headed, determined, from stable to stable, with bucket in hand, against the inevitable flow.

Then, one day, struck out on the sky, the crude unnatural sound of a car, cutting a path through the empty field, coming to rest in the yard. Bucket in hand, an old woman watched, with a staunch dog stood to her side.

A car door opened, and a girl climbed out.

Her hair was thick and clasped in bright bunches. Her face was round, and slightly pale. Her eyes were blue; her nose was snubbed; her lips were smilingly pink. Her clean white dress was patterned with flowers. She seemed about ten years old. She stood in the courtyard and looked at the woman, uncertain of what to do next.

Hello.
Hello.
Would you like to come and look at the field?
All right.
Here. Come and sit on the gate. That's right. Now, what can you see?
I can't see anything.
At the bottom there. Out of sight. There's a cow. Do you like animals?
A bit.
That's lucky. We've got a few animals here.
What have you got?

I've got a dog, a cat, and that cow. Have you got any animals?

No.

Well, I hope you'll like mine. They're all very friendly. I'll let you meet them. Now, would you like some tea?

Yes, please.

I'm your aunt, by the way. Well, sort of your aunt.

The old woman reached to take the girl's hand, and together they strolled inside to the kitchen. A Labrador hobbled up to the girl, wagging its tail and laying its chin, tired and grey, in her lap. A tea-cosy cat sat alone on the dresser, its eyes all-seeing like saucers. The old woman seated the girl at the table; she followed her gaze as she looked round the room. She gave her jam scones, with a dollop of cream. Milk came from a pot in the fridge.

Did you make these scones?

Yes. Do you like them?

They're lovely.

The cream comes straight from the cow.

Could you teach me how to make scones?

Of course. I'd love to. Do you want to see around the farm first though?

All right.

Outside, in the courtyard, the old woman showed her all of the buildings. They ambled alongside a long brick façade that adjoined the farmhouse and was fronted with doors – each of which led to an empty room. Beside one, the old woman paused and rested, pressing her weight on the frame. At the end of the stables were garage doors. And on the other side of the yard was a split-level barn.

Within the gloom of its opened entrance, the rusting shapes of unused machines grew out from a pocket of weeds. Beyond was a building woven with ivy, with two sliding doors stood facing each other – one which led out into the field, the other into the yard. Here, she brought the cow to be milked. And beside it, here was a gate. The old woman showed the girl how it opened. Then they walked together round to an orchard that was tangled and buried in nettles and thorn.

Are those plums?
Yes. Do you like them?
I love them.
Why don't you climb up and get one?
Can you pick it for me?
Yes. There we are.
And those. Are they cooking apples?
That's right.
You make chutney. I know. You make apple pie.
Yes, I do.
It's delicious, isn't it? You make delicious apple pie. The best in the world. I know.
Well, some people like it. Is that what you'd like to do?
Yes please. I'd like that so much.

The old woman looked at the girl. Her eyes were innocent and bright. She was smiling timidly at her aunt, filled with wonder but shy. She was shivering for feeling the breeze. The girl took hold of the old woman's hand, nestling close to the side of her apron as if to keep from the cold. The old woman felt her fragile warmth – the press of her body against her own. She could feel the intimacy of the girl. She hugged it, breathing it in.

After supper, the old woman showed the girl to her bedroom, which was on the ground floor next to the kitchen. She crossed to a window set high in the wall – a small window scarcely two feet square – and closed the drapes on the glass. Then she sat the girl on the bed in her nightdress; she opened her case and unpacked her clothes, hanging and folding, and smiling her joy. They chatted of schools, and hobbies, and friends. Of cakes, and cities, and books. When all her clothes had been put in the drawers, the old woman came and sat on the bed. They sat and they stared into each other's eyes, searching for something unknown. The girl put her arms around the old woman; she hugged her, burying her head in her lap. For a while, it was just the two of them there. Then the old woman rose and turned off the light; she closed the door before leaving the room.

The girl slept until it was late. She rose, got dressed, and washed her face. She greeted her aunt with a kiss. In the kitchen they ate their breakfast together, chatting and smiling and watching each other. All morning the girl was the old woman's shadow; after lunch they drove into town. That day established a new routine. In the days that followed they practised it, until they had made just as they wanted. Perfect just as it was. To begin with, the old woman set the girl tasks – pick all the blackcurrants, brush out the barn – wanting to know she was busy. The girl was keen to oblige. She liked to be of help round the house – tidying, washing, sweeping, cleaning – but liked it more when they worked together, and liked it most just being together, when all their work had been done. A fondness grew between the two: the old woman sensing the girl's affection, the girl desiring her love.

They were both fulfilled by their shared routine. The old woman felt a selfish joy steal through her skin and lodge in her soul, filling an aching emptiness – a barren spot that was buried so deep she had never dared face it or own it. She felt it in the girl's morning kiss; she felt it when holding her hand in the street; she felt it when hugging goodnight. The girl's gentle voice, her laughter, her pleasure sliced through the old woman's flesh to her core, exposing the years of loneliness, and flooding her heart with its bliss. She felt both rapture and fear for sensing how strong it was, and how pure. Love, not known, now known, oppressed her. A love returned with no demand. So complete and yet so simple that it entirely consumed and confused her. She let its bounty wash right through her, cleansing, restoring her soul. And, as she took that generous love, she freely gave of the same.

There was only one corner of the old woman's mind that stood aloof from the girl. A distant echo locked inside that taunted her, saying love was illusion, love was false and simply indulgence, love was transient and cruel. Love wants the things it cannot get; love tires of what it has.

Prompted by that inner voice, as if to test how strong that love, she took the girl out to the yard and pointed to the Judas tree. Age had warped its sturdy boughs, and wind had forced its honest trunk to lean at angles to the ground. Her love demanded proof. Her love desired the girl to climb. It watched her pull her fearful body up towards the lowest branch, and sit there clutching at the truck, afraid of climbing more. Her love desired the girl to swim. It guided her towards the beach, and watched her shying from the waves and shrinking from the cold. Her love desired the girl to explore. It walked her down the rolling field and pressed her crawl beneath the wire towards a ruined house. It urged her cut between the thorns, to scale the broken layers of slate, to sit atop the wall. It watched the girl look back at her with timorous, frightened, wind-cried eyes – so keen to give, so loath to do – to reach towards her aunt and beg to hide within her warming hug, to feel the solace of her arms. And, though she felt her love was strong, the aunt knew from the child's response her love demanded more.

When they had finished their supper each night – once the girl's endless chatter had come to a close, and her bright eyes were weary and tired of the day – she lay in bed with her aunt beside her, listening to stories of old.

Her aunt spoke of a child who was reckless and wild, who hid in the hedges, who crawled through the mud, who hung from the branches high up in a tree. An untamed child, who swam in the sea, who flew with the wind, who danced through the reeds in the ley. A child who was fed from the bosom of nature – who arose with the dawn and returned with the dusk – embraced by the land, and the sea, and the ley. She spoke of a time when that child would sit on the walls of a ruin, at the top of a tree, on the rusting bars of a gate – all day – drinking life in with her eyes. When she swam out far in the restless ocean, her head a dot in the waves. When she strode round the cliff – at its very edge – carelessly brushing a path through the gorse. When she slipped down the field at the first blush of dawn; when she was engulfed by the ley. And she spoke of a creature who lived in the reeds, who spread thin nets to capture the birds. She spoke of the rumours that he was there still – living and sleeping within the reedbed, without ever venturing out.

The girl let the words wash round in her mind, like fairy tales that could brighten her dreams when she closed her eyes and gave herself up to the simple succour of sleep. She loved the old woman; she loved her dearly. For the strength that she felt in her warm embrace, for the comfort that smiled from the walls of her home.

The girl slept soundly, cocooned in the folds of the old woman's love. There was only one corner of her mind which stood fast and kept her from sleep. A distant echo locked inside, which reminded her of a single deed – one simple deed left undone. A deed that stood between her and her aunt, rendering her happiness less than complete. She heard it being mouthed in her mind. And then, when alone – when seeming alone – she would sometimes hear it being mouthed by a living creature which slithered towards her – which crept from a corner as if to torment her – which stared at her with its lidless eyes. She wished she was able to deny its being. To refute and refuse it was real. She wished she was able to stem its demands. But, instead, each day it grew more insistent; chastising her for what lay undone, threatening her for not doing. However close she hugged the old woman, she could see beyond – just over her shoulder – to that other creature that stirred in the shadows, that never came forward nor went away. The girl wasn't brave enough to fight it, nor strong enough to fend off its challenge. Hers was the body and mind of a child; a thing that was wrought of pure virtue.

So came a day when she stood alone in the heart of the sun-spoilt field. She had never been so far from the farm, and never before on her own. She wore a dark jacket, and a grey woollen cap. A gentle breeze blew in from the sea, mocking her, making her eyes fill with tears.

The girl walked down the slope to the fence. She cut through the gaps at the base of the hedges; she crossed the fields till she came to a dune. The wire fell away, and in front of her was a body of reed, with a track leading off to its side. She felt the keen wind snatching her hair; she felt the salt air stinging her neck; she felt the fear of the wailing reeds. In that moment, she felt so alone. She wished the old woman was close beside her, holding her hand and feeding her warmth. She raised her eyes to the farm. All she could see was a motionless figure stood by a hedge between the two fields, urging her on from afar.

She lowered her eyes and started out, stumbling down the uneven track till she came to the place she was told.

She found the mark – a pile of stones – on the bank at the fringe of the ley. She looked at the darkening reeds before her, twisting their agonised stems. They rose, dense and tall, like a living wall, threatening over her head. If she were to enter, they would crowd in upon her, and then they would steal her away. They would squeeze the air from her lungs; they would cut her arms and legs till she bled; they would seek to strangle her with their tassels; they would thrash her, beating her into the water. She would sink in its depths; she would surely drown; and, as she fell through the brackish liquid, all she would see was a sliver of sky closed out by the traitorous reeds.

The girl stood facing the ley. The awesome, venomous mass of reeds. Its curling, threatening scream of hate. She knew she shouldn't be here. They didn't want her; they wouldn't yield. Every instinct told her not to go on. It was only the terror that made her reach out, clutching the reeds and prising them open, staring in past their stems.

In front of her was a stream of brown water, with a lattice of channels beyond. Between each stream was a narrow path, crafted of bridges made of bent reeds, leading into the heart. She needed to jump across the first stretch to reach the bridges beyond. From somewhere, deep within her subconscious, from whispered words from when she was born, she knew it was safe to go on. Though all she could see was the pitiless water, stagnant and depthless, waiting for her. Willing her into its deeps.

She closed her eyes and jumped. For seconds, she felt herself in the air – half flying, half swimming, and sliced by the reeds – uncertain of where she would fall. And now she was no longer moving. She was not in the water, but not on the land. Not dry, nor wet, but somewhere between. She cautiously opened her eyes. She had landed awkwardly on the bridge. It gave with her weight, and yet it held her. It yielded slightly under her feet, as if she was floating on air. Yet it held her. She looked at the reeds, squeezed up to her sides. They clattered and clamoured and cursed at the girl, row after row, in their millions.

The girl felt sick. She wished this was ended. She wished this had never begun. She took a leap to the next stump of bridge, and from there she leapt to the next. Each time she crossed a small course of water. Now she was deep in the ley. All about her the reeds were bristling; they were crowding around and jostling her. The sound of their hate was immense. Hurriedly, she looked for two posts, rising high of the crests. She looked for a fine stretch of netting. She told herself that she wouldn't despair; she would summon her strength and stay calm. But mostly, she persuaded herself that once this was done, she would be back in the field, back in the old woman's arms.

Ahead of her she could see a pole rising up through the delicate tassels, stark against the sheer sky. She steered towards it. And there she found a scatter of stones, marking the chosen spot in the reeds. She slipped behind their wall and crouched down. Low in the seething mass around her; low in the premature dusk that blackened the sulking bed of the ley. Above her, the sky was deepening red, stained with the blood of the day. In front of it was a lattice of webbing, softer than silk and lighter than air, seeming to capture the clouds. Once or twice, she could hear a thud – the strangest of sudden unnatural noises – as something shivered the net. And then all she heard was the bleakest of cries. The sound of liberty lost.

The girl closed her ears to the noise. She closed down her body and stifled her breathing. She tried to wash her mind of the thought she was sitting on a thatch of bent reed, and it was that alone that held her from drowning. The living wall about her shuddered, seeming to mimic her fear. She hugged herself close in her dark green jacket, waiting for something to come.

Now she could hear another noise. A swish in the reeds that wasn't the wind. She could feel the tremor of feet on the bridges as an eager creature came on. Then, almost as soon as she first heard the noise, she saw a shadow – a man on the path – coming at her through the reeds. As he approached the spot where she lay, he turned towards the billowing net. With his back to her, she could see him working, plucking and untangling the web with his hand. When he reached the end of the line of netting, the man came out from behind the reed. The girl stood up. She stood still. She was scarcely three feet in front of the man, on the path that led to the bank.

She had not been told what the man would look like. She had not rehearsed what would happen from here. She had blocked all thought from her mind. In the hope that, like a desperate nightmare, the day would scare it away.

Before her now was a man, dressed in green, with a bag slung over his shoulder. He was slight and awkward, and his left arm was limp, like the broken wing of a bird. In the circling dusk of the sorrowful reeds, he looked more a ghost than a man. She thought he might speak, for his lips seemed to part. For a second only – from a look in his eyes – she thought he knew who she was.

Now was the time she needed to speak, though that was all that she knew –

I want to see your snake.

He stared at her. Staring in silence. Then, of a sudden, he turned. He turned and fled, he thrashed at the reeds, his flayed limbs helpless against them. He went to their core, with a madness, a haste, blind to the bridges beneath his feet, blind to the paths in his way. She saw the ley come to life, clutching his arms in its callous grasp, tightening its hold on his legs. Cackling while dragging him down.

Then she could see him no more. As if the man had been swallowed within. She heard the sound of a body falling, not on a bridge and not in the water, but somewhere still deeper and darker. A noise as if nothing could break that fall. Then only a silence sinking about her. Not even the sound of the whispering reeds. Nothing. Now only one sound. Her sound. The sound of her tears. And, as she cried, she could taste their salt, bitter-sweet in her mouth.

The girl climbed carefully over the bridges, until she was safe on the bank. In the husk of twilight, she followed the track till the fence sank into the dune. Then she came back into the field. An earth-hedge lay, like a slumbering snake, massive and threatening before her. Round its corner a darkened figure slid out of the silence and took her hand. The girl looked into her mother's face, seeing her eyes were focused elsewhere – on somewhere far in the distance. Following her gaze, the girl could see the huge red sun – a thick blood red – sinking into the sea. Night was stealing up the valley; it was creeping over the hills. The sun slipped low, washing the waves with its fiery glow, staining the heads of the reeds. Tinting their tassels in amber and gold, as if the ley was on fire.

They walked together up through the field, past the gate, and into the yard. The girl could foresee what was going to happen. She didn't want to witness it, but she knew. She followed her mother to where the old woman was hunched and scratching at weeds with her hands.

We're going home now.

The old woman straightened herself with effort. She looked into the other's inscrutable eyes –

You will come back.
No.
She will come back.
Maybe.
She will. You owe it to her. It is over for you, but for her this is only the beginning. Both for her and for me.
As you wish.

In the trailing strands of the weary dusk, the old woman watched them enter the farmhouse. She watched them carry their bags to the car. She shuffled over towards the mother, standing before her but not quite touching. She wished her goodbye for a final time. Then the old woman looked at the girl. She looked at the child with her watery eyes staring up from a pale, pale face. She took the girl in her arms. She hugged her, she kissed her, she stroked her cheek. But she didn't think of saying goodbye.

Instead, she wished her goodnight. Goodnight till the morning. Till a new dawn, a new life was born. A life they could share, they could build together. A life where both might find love. She squeezed the magical power of her thoughts into the girl's fragile frame. She held the girl close, in the hug of someone who knows herself to be loved without question. Utterly, unconditionally. She felt that same love being breathed from the girl: entering her, warming her, filling her soul. It was the essence of life. It was life itself. That is the moment we secretly live for. Nothing can take it away.

The old woman held the girl's face in her hand. For a moment, it was just the two of them, there on their own, by themselves. They smiled. Then the girl got into the car, and was driven away, turning her back on the ley.

Earth. The body of land a curvaceous shape clothed with irregular fields. A rainbow of green, windswept and raw, close-fitted around its arching shoulders, its ribs, the mould of its neck. Broken by clumps of crooked bush, by hunchbacked trees and hedges hewn from the soil. Water. A teeming world unseen beyond the splintered teeth of the rock. Washing, ceaseless, against the land, melting into liquid ether as it stretches out beyond sight. Shapeless, yet matching every shape. Restless, resistless, colourless. Forming itself into infinite beings for elusive fractions of time. Wind. Fire. The ley, couched in the valley of the body of earth, its head in the lap of its mother, the sea. A shock of sudden pools and potholes; of natural traps and snares. Thrashed by the wind, burned by the sun, mocked by the chattering reeds.

Summer bears autumn, bears winter. The sea spews its salt in the mouth of the ley, forcing it open to drink of it deep, till the sullen waters are stirred into life. Leaden skies empty their spiteful load as they meet with the desolate land. Rain spins off the polished earth; it chases down the furrowed fields till the valley is choked and is drowned. The reeds bend in agony, creased by the onslaught, screaming a foul-mouthed wretchedness, weighted down by the pain. Morning's fingers claw at the land, shivering a light which never quite warms, which never quite brings into life. At times, uneasy stillness falls; a coolness, a freshness, an emptiness; an absence having no end. Then, in that greyness of flaccid unbeing, the world is undone. The ley seems senseless, disused. Though still it chants a rosary through tight, invisible lips. Still it breathes, and still it waits. Alive. Forever awake.

Colours shift and clouds roll through; the winds pick up and die. Then a crack in the cloud. The faintest of rays from a searching sun caressing the fabric of earth. Somewhere, a snowdrop. A noise in the fields of nature feeling her way. A robin perched low on a Judas tree. Damp early mornings, and a shimmering sea, sucking its breath through its teeth. The dawn spilling its blush on the idle darkness, chasing away its grey tails.

The land rears up as if to embrace it. The reeds are burnished a bloodied red as the mist burns off their brittle backs, as they meet with the rays of the sun. They lisp a shivering song with no words, while dancing their trance in the wind.

The reedbed thickens, ecstatically green. The sun scorches its tips and bronzes its curtains, setting the valley on fire. The reeds are pregnant with the promise of life, sweating and sighing a warm embrace between the thighs of the fields. Though the brackish waters that sulk at their base are hidden forever – hiding their secrets and all within them from the probing gaze of the sun. Birds re-enter the crowded haven, seeking retreat and safe harbour. Nests are made amidst the haste of furious feeding, feuding, existing. The ley is vibrant, pulsing with being, filled with the urgent chorus of life.

Not earth nor water, but somewhere between. A land forged from the bowels of the earth and sculpted into miraculous being. A borderland, a micro world. A part of the real world, living apart. Free from the clutch of curious man. A paradise, as much as a prison. The power and the glory. Bowing to seasons, to wind and to fire, to the shocks that nature thrusts upon it. Host to a universe entire. A labyrinth of twisting reed, where creatures search and stumble blind. A place of death, of things once drowned, of things that have decayed. An industrious, awesome isolation. A splendid soulful solitude. Living, thriving, surviving, dying, in a constant cycle of renewal. Feeding and feasting off its own. Ageless and timeless and without end. For ever and ever.

This is the ley.

打蛇不死，后患无穷

Unless you beat a snake to death,
it will cause endless trouble in future

**The
Children's
Society**

It is a painful fact that many children and young people in Britain today are still suffering extreme hardship, abuse and neglect. Too often their problems are ignored and their voices unheard. Now it is time to listen and to act.

The Children's Society is a national charity that runs local services, helping children and young people when they are at their most vulnerable, and have nowhere left to turn.

It also campaigns for changes to laws affecting children and young people, to stop the mistakes of the past being repeated in the future.

Its supporters around the country fund its services and join its campaigns to show children and young people they are on their side.

All royalties from the sale of this book
go towards the work of The Children's Society